Escape From Eden

Escape
From Eden

Dayle Courtney

**Illustrated by
John Ham**

STANDARD PUBLISHING
Cincinnati, Ohio   2712

Thorne Twins Adventure Books

1 Flight to Terror
2 Escape From Eden
3 The Knife With Eyes
4 The Ivy Plot
5 Operation Doomsday
6 Omen of the Flying Light

Library of Congress Cataloging in Publication Data

Courtney, Dayle.
  Escape from eden.

  (Thorne Twins adventure books)
  For 13-19 year olds.
  Summary: Shipwrecked on the Hawaiian island of
Molokai, Eric finds himself the prisoner of the Children
of Eden, a colony ruled by an evil leader who claims to
be the goddess of volcanoes.
  [1. Cults—Fiction. 2. Hawaii—Fiction] I. Ham,
John. II. Title. III. Series: Courtney, Dayle. Thorne
Twins adventure books.
PZ7.C83158Es   [Fic]   81-5710
ISBN 0-87239-467-0   AACR2

Copyright © 1981, The STANDARD PUBLISHING Company, Cincinnati, Ohio.
A division of STANDEX INTERNATIONAL Corporation. Printed in U.S.A.

Contents

1   Volcano   7

2   Lost at Sea   25

3   Shipwreck   40

4   The Gods of Eden   56

5   Overnight Guest in Eden   69

6   Pursuit   81

7   Noelani   93

8   Descent Toward Death   104

9   The Plant Puzzle   114

10   The Mystery of Eden   126

11   The Disappearance of Dr. Thorne   136

12   Journey Toward Terror   151

13   Return to Eden   161

14   Tsunami   176

1 • Volcano

Under the calm Pacific waters south of the Hawaiian Islands the earth heaved suddenly. Tiny, jewel-bright fish scattered as a coral reef trembled and broke apart. Deeper, a shark chasing a school of fat yellow anglers lost them when a sudden swirl of hot mud spit up from a fissure, and hid them. In the dark depths, twelve hundred feet down, a gold coral tree split and crumbled. For a while the earth was still. Then another tremor jolted a squid from its hiding place in a cave, as molten rock from the earth's center spilled over the sea floor.

On the island of Oahu, Eric Thorne thought he felt a slight trembling of the pavement. Was it caused by the stream of cars passing by along Kalakaua Avenue, or the double-decker bus slowing at the curb to let out a crowd of tourists?

Nothing to get upset about, he concluded.

The main street of Waikiki was crowded with sun-tanned people in bright Hawaiian shirts and muumuus.

A few of the girls looked twice as they passed sixteen-year-old Eric, tall, dark-haired, handsome features, with bronzed skin and the lithe body of an athlete. Any other time Eric would have enjoyed the attention, but at this moment he had his mind on one thing only—food.

He turned into the International Marketplace and brightened at the pungent smells of cooking oils and spices. After a morning of surfing, he was hungry. It was not imagination that he could hear his stomach rumbling.

But was that rumbling only his stomach? It couldn't be. Along with the low rumble the ground was beginning to shake. People in the marketplace stopped their shopping. They glanced around, looking bewildered.

"Pele! Pele is angry! Pele! Pele is angry! Pele . . ."

The swelling chant came from an old Hawaiian merchant under the great banyan tree at the center of the plaza.

"Pele? You mean the volcano goddess?" Eric asked him.

The white-haired man nodded and continued his chanting.

"Does Pele often get angry?" Eric asked. But the old man, head to one side and listening intently, had tuned him out. The half-formed, miniature outrigger the old Hawaiian had been whittling dangled forgotten in his hand.

A volcano?

Eric hesitated. He knew there were active volcanoes in the Hawaiian chain of islands, but were there any here on Oahu? He could think only of Diamond Head, and that had lain dormant for ages. It wasn't extinct, he knew. Was it possible that the great black rock he had been surfing around all morning, with buildings crowding its sloping sides, could now be preparing to erupt? It had seemed to be a symbol of Oahu—serene and unchanging.

"Pele is angry—"

Brushing off the woodcarver's words as just some of the local superstition, Eric headed for the wooden stairway that led to Trader Vic's restaurant.

And then he saw her.

She stood talking to a man outside a souvenir stand only a few feet away. A slender girl in a pink-flowered muumuu, whose glistening black hair was caught back over one ear with a white ginger blossom. She was holding flower leis on her arm and was smiling at the man who had selected one to buy. Yes, it had to be her! The familiar beauty of her features pierced Eric with a stab of recognition. He called out her name.

"Noelani!"

She whirled to look at him, her dark brown eyes wide with surprise, and for a moment it seemed that the marketplace grew empty and silent while they looked at each other.

"Eric Thorne!" Her voice was a cry of happiness as she moved toward him. "What are you doing here in Hawaii?"

She was close enough now for Eric to catch the faint scent of ginger and to make him forget momentarily about his hunger—and even the strange rumblings of the earth.

"I just got here yesterday," Eric said. "My dad's here on an assignment for the International Agricultural Foundation. I'm spending the summer with him."

Noelani smiled up at him, her cheeks dimpling.

"You're even better looking than your recent pictures."

"So are you." He grinned back at her. "But what are

you doing here on Oahu, in Waikiki? Don't you live on Molokai?"

"I do, but I come over here every couple of weeks to sell leis to the tourists." She held out her arm so he could see the flower garlands arrayed on it. "They help raise money for the Colony." She picked out a lei of tiny purple orchids and draped it around his neck. "Aloha," she said with the customary kiss on each cheek. "Welcome to Hawaii. A present for you from me."

"Thank you," Eric said, pleased.

"It seems funny, doesn't it?" Noelani went on. "I mean, how we recognized each other right away. We haven't seen each other for two years."

Eric couldn't believe how beautiful she was. He wondered how he could have missed noticing that at the White House Rose Garden reception when she was fourteen—even in the school uniform she was wearing then. On that occasion he and twin sister Alison had been among the teenagers invited to entertain the group from the famous Kamehameha school in Hawaii.

Noelani had come to the mainland with one of the schools. Later when she saw his photo in a magazine, along with an article about a tennis tournament he had won, she had written to him with a refreshing naturalness. Her letter had been unlike any other fan mail he had ever received.

Noelani never referred to his connection with Gramps. Eric wondered if she even realized that E. Bradford Thorne, the Vice President of the United States, was his grandfather. To this lovely girl, the fact that they had been introduced at the White House event was reason enough to write.

Eric answered her letter and she wrote again. Her letters began to include glowing news about the Eden

Colony on the island of Molokai where she was born. She told him she left the English church school to become a Colony member. Then she had enclosed poems she had written, and photographs of herself in colorful muumuus with ginger blossoms in her hair.

Just like she looked today.

"I tried to phone you last night," Eric said, "but the operator didn't have a listing for Eden."

"I know. We don't have any phones there."

"I even thought about renting a boat to go over to Molokai and visit you."

She looked up at him, frowning. "Oh, I don't think you could."

"Why not?"

She seemed reluctant to answer. "Well, they have to screen everybody who goes there. You know, interviews and things like that."

Eric was surprised. In her letters she'd described Eden as a wonderful place full of friendly people. Now she made it sound either very exclusive or very unfriendly.

"Why do they do that?" he asked her.

She shook her head and glanced around. Her voice was almost a whisper.

"I can't talk about it right now."

"Well I was just going to have lunch, over there at Trader Vic's. Why don't you come with me?"

She looked frightened now.

"Oh, no. I couldn't." She backed away from him.

Eric was baffled.

"Why not?"

She was looking around nervously as though searching for someone. Eric followed her gaze to a man rising from a table at an outside cafe. The man walked into the crowd before Eric could see him clearly.

Suddenly, with a loud, rumbling roar, the earth gave a great heave. Somebody screamed. A branch of the huge banyan quivered over Eric's head and then crashed to the ground in front of him, debris falling everywhere. A slab of grass roof from one of the little stalls thudded to the pavement between Eric and Noelani, with wind chimes and china and pieces of glass tinkling after it.

Something slammed Eric's shoulder and he winced with the pain of it, but didn't look to see what it might have been. He kept his eyes on the place where Noelani had stood, his vision obscured, now, by the dust and debris falling between them. A pair of electrical wires, torn loose, sparked perilously close to his head as he backed away from them, smelling the acrid scent, hearing the cracking and crashing of the frail little structures throughout the marketplace.

People scurried in every direction, shouting and shrieking, while parts of buildings crumbled and dropped about them.

"Noelani!" Eric yelled to be heard over the holocaust. "Are you all right? Where are you?"

He strained to hear her answer, but there was too much noise. Somehow he had to find her. He had to be sure she wasn't hurt—get her out of this dangerous place to safety. He tried to climb over the heap of rubble that had fallen between them, but it was loose and unsteady so that he only slipped and slid while pieces of glass and wood pelted down on him. Finally he gave up trying, and looked for a way to get around the debris that had fallen where he'd last seen her.

Someone was shrieking behind him.

Turning, he saw a woman sprawled on the floor of what had once been a jewelry shop. Now it was a mass of wreckage. She lay on her face, in obvious agony, a heavy

13

glass case full of jumbled trinkets pinning the lower half of her body so that she couldn't move. Eric saw no one else near her. He would have to help her before he could continue his search for Noelani. Eric ran to the screaming woman, knelt beside her, and forced his voice to stay calm. "It's all right. I'll get you out of there."

"Hurry. Please, hurry. Please—"

The woman stopped her weak struggles and lay still, while Eric strained at the heavy case. Two of its supporting legs had broken. With a huge effort he managed to heave it off her body, shoving it in the other direction so that it crashed harmlessly. Then he helped the woman to stand.

"Are you badly hurt?" he asked her.

"I don't know." She leaned heavily on his arm. "My leg. Feels broken."

He looked at her bare legs, already black and blue, and saw a trickle of blood coming from a gash in one of them.

"Mary!" A balding man hurried toward them, shoving aside the rubble that blocked his path. "I've been looking all over for you!" He glanced down at her injured legs. "Oh, Mary! Are you all right?"

The woman began to sob. The man held her in his arms and thanked Eric for his help.

"Can you take care of her now?" Eric asked him. "Do you need help getting her outside?"

"No—no, thank you. We'll manage."

Eric went back through the now nearly empty marketplace. He could hear sirens in the distance. What had caused all this destruction? Was the center of the quake here in the marketplace? Was all the island in a turmoil? He thought about his dad waiting for him at the hotel as he clambered over heaps of broken glass and fallen

14

beams calling Noelani's name, praying she would be unhurt.

A few people still huddled in whatever shelter remained standing. Some wandered aimlessly, calling out for friends or relatives. Many had cuts and bruises and bleeding wounds that gave Eric a vision of Noelani lying, broken and bloody, under one of these heaps. He searched every corner of the marketplace, but at last he knew he could not find her. She might have panicked and run out to the street without trying to contact him. This puzzled him. But maybe he'd see her outside.

The street was a river of people, all going in the same direction, away from Diamond Head. Eric looked toward it and saw a black cloud of dark vapor rising toward the sky. The smell of sulfur was in the air. Even though he could not see anything except the darkening cloud, Eric sensed what was happening.

Diamond Head was erupting!

He scanned the faces of the people racing past him, looking, hoping. But there was little chance of finding Noelani in this multitude of people all racing for safety away from the smoldering mountain. Eric forced himself to remain calm, afraid the crowd would turn into a trampling, raging mob. He stepped back from the street into the shelter of a doorway, and tried to decide what to do.

Eric shivered as he looked up at the cloud hanging over Diamond Head. The dark cloud was drifting out to sea blown by the strong trade winds.

Should he wait and run for safety after the crowd was gone? But where was safety? Where were these people going? To the beaches, maybe, to find boats to take them off the island. Or maybe to the airport. He didn't know. Fear began to grip him. Pulling himself together he reasoned that the first thing to do was to get to the hotel and find his dad. But he didn't want to get caught in that swarm of scared people. He glanced into the shop behind him, saw that it was empty, and ran through it. Yes—there was a back door. He dodged through it into the nearly empty alley. Finally he was on Kuhio Street, racing toward the hotel.

Here the damage did not seem to be serious. There were little groups of people on the streets, looking up at the dark cloud hanging over Diamond Head. Some were gathered on balconies and in windows, but none of them seemed to be trying to leave. He slowed to a trot and went on to the hotel.

A few people were in the lobby, gathered around a radio. A calm voice was telling them not to panic, to clear the area as soon as possible, that Diamond Head was erupting. The doors of the elevator opened, drowning out the sound of the voice, and Eric rode to the top floor.

Dr. Randall Thorne was in the room of his suite that served as his office, putting papers into a briefcase. He looked agitated, but seemed relieved to see his son.

"Eric, thank God you're here! I figured it was better to stay here than to go looking for you. I was afraid you were still surfing out by Diamond Head when this awful thing happened."

"No, Dad, I'm fine. I was in the marketplace. Everything okay here?"

"Some broken china—a few pictures shaken off the walls. Nobody hurt that I know of. Television reception is out." He turned up the volume on the radio behind his desk, but there was only silence now.

"It's tuned to the emergency station. They put out bulletins as they come in, but I'm afraid nobody has any clear idea of what to do yet. They're telling people to leave the area and stay calm. That's about all."

"I'm glad Alison changed her plans to come this week," Eric said as he collapsed in a chair, suddenly very tired. "Guess the last thing anyone expected was for Diamond Head to blow its top. Will we have to leave?"

His father nodded. "There'll be a helicopter waiting for us at the airport at two o'clock to take us to Molokai."

"Molokai?"

"Yes. I made the arrangements last week, before any of this happened. I need to go out to the *Puu O Hoku* Ranch there. I'm making a study of the nutritional quality of the ground cover their cattle graze on. I was going to go alone, but now both of us had better go." Dr. Thorne fastened his briefcase.

"We're fortunate we have a way to get off this island before anything more disastrous happens. We'll leave as soon as you pack up."

Eric threw things quickly into his bag. Within minutes he and his father were in the car, making their way through the crowds toward the Honolulu airport.

Traffic moved slowly, bumper-to-bumper. A radio advised them to stay calm; that Diamond Head was not yet spilling lava; that there was no immediate danger to life or property; and that emergency vehicles were available to evacuate those in the Waikiki beach area.

"Will we get off before the lava starts spilling out?" Eric asked his father as they drove.

"There's no way to be sure. Diamond Head might be building up to a big eruption in a few hours, or a few days. Then again, it may quiet down and nothing more will happen."

Eric looked down at the crumpled lei of orchids

17

around his neck and thought of Noelani. Where was she? He scanned the occupants of the other cars as they inched along, hoping to see her face, but only strangers' eyes looked back at him. Maybe she was still in the marketplace, injured and deserted. If only he'd been able to find her!

Maybe he should tell his dad he wanted to stay here—to volunteer for one of the rescue teams and search for her at the same time. But he knew that would be useless. Dad wouldn't leave the island without him, and anyway, what could he do? He didn't know his way around Oahu, and he didn't have any search-and-rescue training. He could only hope and pray that she had escaped and was on her way back to Molokai.

Dr. Thorne was a reference bank of information about volcanoes.

"Did you know that these Hawaiian Islands were formed by volcanoes, Eric? They started under the sea, but gradually, over the centuries, the lava flows hardened and built up until they rose above the ocean's surface."

"I've read about it, Dad." Eric hoped his father wouldn't launch into one of his professorial lectures right now. Not while Eric was so worried he could hardly pay attention. He was about to say something when he looked at his father's strained face. On the off chance that his father's classroom voice would have a calming effect on the speaker himself, Eric stifled an objection to the continuing lecture.

"Mauna Loa, on the big island of Hawaii, is the tallest mountain in the world. It's even higher than Mount Everest if you measure from its base on the seafloor. It's more than 31,000 feet high. And just think, it started about a million years ago as a puddle of lava spilling out over the bottom of the sea."

"There's a stalled car up ahead, Dad—"

Dr. Thorne followed the car in front as it straddled the sidewalk to get around the disabled taxi. Pedestrians swarmed into the spaces between stop-and-go traffic.

"The earth's land masses are formed of tectonic plates," his father went on. The voice was more relaxed than the hands on the wheel, Eric noted.

"Huge pieces of land that are always shifting. The friction when they hit against one another causes intense heat in the molten rock under them. That heat causes volcanoes."

Eric sighed. All this information was really more than he wanted to know just now.

Traffic moved forward, then lurched to a sudden stop. Dr. Thorne hit the brakes. "Now what's wrong?" he asked sharply.

Eric stuck his head out of the window to get a better look. "It's okay, Dad. Just jaywalkers trying to crowd in front of the cars." He rolled up the window as the smell of sulfur grew stronger. "So did the Hawaiian volcanoes form on the edge of those plates?"

"No, actually they lie in the middle of a plate, but when it moved over a particularly hot spot in the earth's mantle, a row of volcanoes was—was created that eventually—eventually became these islands and—"

Driving was desperate now.

They were coming near the airport, and the traffic had slowed almost to a halt. Dr. Thorne managed to get the rental car turned into a side street where he could park it. He would call an associate later to return it, he had decided. As they hurried toward the landing field, Eric glanced at his watch and noted that it was ten past two. The place was surging with anxious people searching for friends, family and a way to leave the island.

Every possible kind of aircraft was warming up on the field. There seemed to be no order here at all, with people milling over the runways, trying to board anything that would fly. Carts heaped with passengers and baggage scurried among them. Eric climbed up on one of the landing ramps to look for the white helicopter with "International Agricultural Foundation" in maroon lettering on its tail. Eric spotted it and they headed through the crowd, out to the helicopter pad.

The pilot was waiting in the cabin. He started the motor as they climbed in. "Dr. Thorne, if you'd been five minutes later, I would have had to take other passengers and leave," he said with obvious relief to have his scheduled passengers aboard. "This whole island's going crazy."

"Thank you for waiting." Dr. Thorne took one of the seats behind the pilot. "We don't mind sharing with other passengers if you want to take some."

Eric looked through the Plexiglas bubble at the people standing around them. Two teenage girls watched them wistfully, suitcases in hand. A woman with a small child stood near them, and a short distance away, a group of adults stood hoping for a chance to board anything that would take them away.

"How many will this copter hold?" Eric asked the pilot.

"Four—one more besides ourselves."

"That woman with the little girl," Eric pointed out. "Couldn't she hold the child on her lap?"

The pilot nodded.

"I guess so. But it's not just a matter of seating them. The chopper can't take too much weight." He beckoned to the woman and child. "Come on," he called to them through the open door. "We're headed for Molokai. If you want, we can take you there."

With a smile, the woman grabbed the little girl's hand and headed toward them. But just as she reached the door Eric held open for her, two men jostled her roughly aside, and before anyone could stop them, they were crowding inside.

"Hey!" the pilot shouted. "What do you think you're doing?"

Eric, who was closest to them, tried to bar their way.

The first man gave Eric a shove and with one swift motion, pulled a gun from a hidden holster and aimed it at the pilot.

"We're going with you, or somebody's going to get hurt."

Turning to Eric and his father he snarled, "Now if you want this fellow to live, you won't interfere. We ain't anxious to get buried under no lava." He turned to the pilot. "Start this thing up and get out of here."

Eric's first thought was to get that gun from the man who held it. Dr. Thorne seemed to guess what was in his mind, for he laid a hand on Eric's arm.

"You can't reason with blind force, Son. Don't try."

The man with the gun, red-haired and red-faced, motioned Eric out of his seat beside the pilot, then held it forward so the other man could get in the back beside Dr. Thorne.

"You watch this guy, Jim," he said. "I'll sit right next to the fly-boy, here. And you—" he motioned to Eric, "can squeeze right in here beside me where I can keep an eye on you. Don't get any ideas about trying anything."

Eric knew he couldn't fight a gun. Stunned and angry he closed the door beside him as the aircraft began to rise. The little girl and her mother looked bewildered as the helicopter lifted. Maybe she'd tell the police, he thought, but then he knew that was useless. The police and all the other authorities on Oahu were probably busy with the emergency.

The pilot was talking to the two hijackers.

"You're breaking the law, you know. There's a big penalty for hijacking an aircraft."

"Yeah?" the red-haired man laughed. "Well, this gun can give you a bigger penalty if you don't get us out of here. Fast."

"This aircraft isn't meant to carry five passengers," the pilot insisted. The extra weight is going to make it unstable."

"You'll find a way to fly it," the man said. "If you can't, we can always dump these other two."

The pilot glared at him, but didn't argue further. He maneuvered the helicopter over the crowded field and soon they were leaving the airport.

"Hey, Nat," the man in the back said. "Take a look at the tourist, here. Dig the lei he's wearing." He poked at Eric's neck as he fondled the garland of flowers Noelani had given him.

The red-haired man turned to look.

"Hey, that's pretty neat."

"I got this from a friend," Eric said. "Go buy your own."

Nat's big hand reached out suddenly and yanked the lei over Eric's head. "I prefer this one. Purple's my favorite color." He draped it around his own neck, patting it.

Eric was sullen. It wasn't worth risking someone getting shot over a flower lei, however sentimental. He couldn't understand their interest in the lei. Maybe these two were just trying to find an excuse to get him to fight. Well, he wouldn't give them the satisfaction. But anger

22

smoldered in him as he watched the swirling clouds out by Diamond Head and kept his mouth shut.

"Hey, look, Nat," the man in the back said, excited. "We're going right past Diamond Head."

Nat narrowed his eyes and spoke to the pilot.

"What are you trying to do?"

"Nothing. We have to go this way to get to Molokai."

The cabin of the helicopter was filled with the stench of sulfur now, and through the clouds, Eric could see the caldera of the volcano below, where a pool of red moved restlessly.

"Hey, look at that!" Nat peered at it. "Let's get a closer look."

"It's too dangerous," the pilot said. "We're carrying too much weight, I told you. We're flying too low now."

"I said we want a closer look."

Nat pressed the gun into the pilot's cheek.

Eric was suddenly furious. This was too much! These men had forced their way into the helicopter, threatened to kill them, and stranded a woman and child. Now they wanted to take a chance on killing them all just for the kicks of seeing the volcano up close. If he moved quickly he might be able to get that gun out of this lunatic's hand.

He braced himself, waited until Nat's attention was entirely on the caldera beneath them, and lunged for the gun with both hands.

He had it! Nat's fingers had slackened on the weapon as he looked down, and Eric had it now. Moving swiftly, he opened the door of the helicopter and tossed it out.

The stunned silence was broken by Nat's bellowing and lashing out at Eric with his fists. In order to defend himself, Eric gave up on trying to fasten the helicopter door. With Nat's hands tightening around his throat,

Eric struggled for every breath, trying desperately to break the man's grip.

"The door—" Dr. Thorne shouted as it swung outward. "Get the door, Eric!"

The helicopter was dropping quickly. Eric could feel the hot blast of air that came through the open door. He felt Nat's hands loosen their hold on his neck, but realized that he was now being shoved backward toward the opening. In a desperate grip, Eric locked his hands around the back of his seat.

"I'm losing control!" he heard the pilot shout.

At that moment the second man, who had Dr. Thorne pinned down in the back seat, sent a crushing blow with his foot to Eric's knuckles, breaking his hold on the back of the seat. Within seconds, Nat delivered a great heave against Eric's left shoulder. Grasping helplessly at the air, Eric felt himself outside the door and falling—falling—falling.

"God help me!" The words of his startled cry plummeted downward with him toward the inferno below. His body was rigid, eyes squeezed shut, as he waited for the end.

2 • *Lost at Sea*

The shock of the cold water was intense. Feet first, Eric stabbed the ocean's surface. Hurtling down into its sudden green silence, down—down—down he went. He felt the force of his fall sending him further and further into the cold darkness.

When, at last, his descent slowed, his mind registered the information that he had fallen into the sea.

"Thank You, God! I'm alive!" he prayed.

Now able to move his arms and legs, Eric turned his face upward, to swim for the air, for the sunshine. His nose and mouth were full of salt water, and his lungs ached when he finally reached the surface. Eagerly he gulped at the air.

As his mind cleared and his numbed senses returned, his first thought was to loosen the tennis shoes that were like lead weights now on his feet. He struggled to pull them off. Then he turned over on his back to float, resting his shocked body.

Eric went down the list of arms, legs, knees, fingers,

toes. They all moved without difficulty.

"Lord, I seem to be all in one piece! Where do we go from here?"

The gentle swells of the ocean cradled his still aching arms. He fought to stay alert and to get his bearings.

His focus returned in time to pick out a speck of white against the cloudy sky. Must be the helicopter flying low over the water, he told himself. Looks like the pilot has regained control of the craft. But I bet the hijackers won't let him search the surface and try to find me.

Eric groaned aloud as he scanned the water in every direction.

Even with the realization of his serious predicament uppermost in his thoughts, his mind returned again and again to the question.

"How did I manage to land in the ocean? I'm sure I was headed for that boiling crater. Amazing!" he felt very grateful and thankful as his breathing became less labored.

The copter must have flown out just past the crater while they were struggling, Eric decided. They must have been flying very low because they seemed to be losing altitude fast. Probably due to the weight of the extra passenger. He now estimated the distance of his fall as not more than fifty feet. It had seemed like miles.

This was not Eric's first brush with death. And now he did not doubt that God had for some purpose extended his life once again.

The water was becoming increasingly choppy. Eric sensed that a strong breeze was now blowing. He turned over and swam a few strokes. A feeling of panic was rising within him.

How far was it to land, he wondered. He was out in the ocean—alone. Eric didn't know for sure how far offshore he really was. He looked for some landmark, but all he could see was water and the cloudy sky that covered the whole of the visible world. And, he figured, nobody but God even knew he was alive. He could drown, or be eaten by sharks!

The thought of sharks convulsed him with fear. His arms and legs propelled him forward aimlessly until he was too tired to go on. He began to struggle to keep his weary body afloat.

But this was no good. He had to keep up his courage. Wasn't it true that panic could kill you quicker than anything? Then he'd better try to calm himself—try to think what to do. He lay on his back again, forcing himself to relax against the water, to let the air in his lungs keep him floating while he rested and considered his situation.

How could he tell which way to go to reach land? The helicopter had been flying toward Molokai, hadn't it? Then he should swim in the direction he'd last seen it going. He must have fallen into the Kaiwi Channel between Oahu and Molokai. That being the case, all he had to do was swim for Molokai.

But that was miles away. He didn't even know how many. Wouldn't it be easier to try to swim back to Oahu which was closer? If he swam in the opposite direction to the helicopter, he'd get back to Waikiki.

No. That was no good. Even if he could find his way back to Oahu, there was still the risk of swimming toward an erupting volcano. Molokai was his only chance. If he took it easy, swimming a bit and then floating a bit to rest himself, he might make it. And wouldn't he soon see some boats? There were dozens of boats in that exodus from Waikiki. Wouldn't they head for Molokai, too, since it was the closest island to Oahu?

27

Encouraged by these thoughts, he began to swim again. When he tired, he floated for a while before swimming on again. It was tough going in the choppy waves. It was hard, too, trying not to think that he might have fallen into the ocean south of Oahu instead of in the channel. If that was the case, then he could swim for a year and never reach land in the vast expanse of the Pacific Ocean. But he'd better not think such thoughts!

After all, God knew where he was. He had asked the Lord to help him. So, Eric decided, I'll just keep in touch with Him. With that, he sent up another prayer and swam on.

Swim and float. Swim and float. One of his favorite sports was fast becoming a serious exercise for survival.

Rising on the swells and falling again in the troughs, eyes shut much of the time to keep out the stinging salt water, Eric counted on the moments when he could rise to watch for a boat that might pick him up.

Swim and float. Swim and float. Think of good things, happy things, he told himself. Things like the smell of Aunt Rose's blueberry pie. The time he and his twin sister Alison had finished off one whole pie while Aunt Rose was out shopping.

"But that's no good to think about," Eric knew. He found no comfort in thoughts like these. "Thinking of food only makes me feel hungry."

He forced himself to think of something else—like the time he swam across Fox Lake last summer, when Mark dared him to do it.

"Hey, you did it then, Eric, and you can keep swimming now with God's help. The ocean's only a big lake— the Lord made it, and He's out here with you!"

Swim and float. Swim and float. Keep thinking of more good things, more happy things.

28

It was while he was body surfing, the waves raising him high enough so that he could see some distance, that he spotted the boat. It was a small sailboat, not far from him, skimming the water like a white seabird.

"A boat! Rescued!" Filled with hope, he shouted and waved his arms before slipping down in a trough between the swells. When he rose the next time, he tried again, but his voice was hoarse from the salt water and his arms weary from constant swimming.

Again and again the waves tossed him about and hid him from the sight of those sailing nearby. The boat raced on past, as though he were not there.

"Come back! Come back!" Eric groaned, feeling the panic rising again. Stunned, he watched the sail disappear in the distance.

Now the ocean seemed even bigger and more menacing. Desperately, he realized the people on board were unable to see him. Perhaps other boats would pass him the same way. He struggled to push away thoughts of the dark, cold depths under him; the big, hungry fish, and the skeletons lying on the bottom with empty eyes, waiting for him to join them.

When Eric's thoughts had calmed a little, he began to reminisce again. "You are twelve years old, Eric, in the big swimming pool at school. You are taking a Red Cross swimming and lifesaving course. The instructor is telling the class to go into the pool with their jeans on! You are first to respond!

"Remember how he showed the class how to take their jeans off while they tread water, and flip them so that the air would fill the legs?"

Eric remembered he had tied each leg in a knot to hold the air inside while he held the waist and used the makeshift life preserver to help keep afloat.

"If you do that now, Eric, you could free your body of the extra weight of the jeans as well as making a signal that another boat could see!"

He got his wallet out of his jeans and put it in his shirt pocket, buttoning the flap. The wet zipper of his jeans didn't want to move, but when it finally did, it caught on the swimming trunks he wore underneath. Controlling his frustration, he managed to move the zipper down and get the pants off, but a wave tossed him so that he took a mouthful of sea water as he did so.

Finally he succeeded in knotting the soaked material. Treading water to free one arm, he flipped the jeans over his head to catch the air that would inflate them.

"It works!" Eric shouted. "It really works!"

As he paddled along behind, the blue legs were standing up in front of him like big, uneven rabbit ears. Their buoyancy eased Eric's weariness in staying afloat. Now when another boat comes along, they will surely see me, he decided.

Eric's gratefulness for the slight improvement in his condition melted into something like a prayer. It was usually Alison who prayed when the going got rough, but this time he was on his own.

"I know You heard me, Lord, back there when I was falling from the helicopter. 'Cause here I am, still alive, and still needing Your help to get me through this one."

Eric continued, "I'm sure You are being bombarded with prayers today from this part of the world, but here's another one, just the same."

Eric ended his petition with the only formal word in it—"Amen." He knew he would go on praying with every bone and muscle in his body. He kept his blue denim sails afloat and called out at intervals to imaginary boats. He refused to think of nightfall.

It seemed as though hours had passed before Eric saw another boat, a white cabin cruiser. He shouted and waved the jeans, and again he had to struggle in the water, taking in mouthfuls of brine. But this time the boat slowed, engine throbbing, and moved in his direction. Soon a life preserver landed in the water near him! They were stopping to pick him up! With a fresh burst of energy, he swam to the life preserver, put it on, and heard a man's voice calling encouragement to him as he was pulled on board.

Eric didn't remember too much for a while after that. He was aware of being wrapped in a blanket, and of a hot liquid going down his throat before he collapsed on a bunk. How good it felt to close his tired, burning eyes!

He dozed fitfully, perhaps even slept. He wasn't sure, but he thought he heard a man's voice, and a woman's voice. And once he felt a warm, furry body push against his hand.

When he finally opened his eyes, he was momentarily confused. Where was he? How had he gotten here? Who were these two people watching him?

"Welcome back to the world. I think you're going to be all right." The woman, small and gray-haired, smiled at him.

The man nodded solemnly. "There's color in his cheeks, Susie, and focus to his eyes. We've got ourselves a live one, for sure."

Eric started to peel off the blanket that shrouded him, but stopped when he realized that was all he was wearing. Something stirred beside him and he looked down, startled, to see a huge white cat lying there beside his water-stained wallet.

The man laughed.

"It's only Popoki, my lad. Cats can always find the

31

most comfortable spot, and in this case it happens to be you. We left her there, thinking she'd help to warm you."

"That's okay. I like cats."

Eric reached out to stroke her, his fingers sinking pleasantly into the thick fur, feeling the vibration of the purring body.

The woman came over to him, holding out a mug.

"Here's something hot to drink."

Eric sipped the tea and glanced around. He was in the cabin of the small cruiser. The motor was silent as they rocked on the waves. As he looked at the man who sat in a chair opposite him and the woman who was taking food from a small chest, an immense feeling of gratitude swelled in his throat.

"You saved my life," Eric said. "Thank you."

The man's tanned face wrinkled as he grinned and held out a calloused hand.

"Our pleasure, my lad. We don't like tourists dying in our Hawaiian paradise. Not at all. You *are* a tourist, aren't you?"

"Yes. My hometown is Ivy, a little college town in Illinois. My dad's working out here on a temporary assignment. I'm Eric Thorne."

"I'm Harry Harley. And that's Susie, my wife." Mr. Harley's eyes twinkled.

"Could you fish out some sandwiches for us? It'll be a while till we get to Molokai at this rate." He turned to Eric. "We've been letting the *Kamalo* drift until you felt better, waiting to hear what's up with you. Feel strong enough to tell us?"

So, between bites of the cheese sandwich that tasted better than anything Eric had ever eaten, he told them what had happened.

32

When he finished, Mrs. Harley looked at her watch.

"You say you left Honolulu airport at two?"

"A little after."

"Well, it's nearly five o'clock now. You were in the ocean for nearly three hours. That's a good long time."

"It seemed like ten!" Eric reflected.

Mr. Harley was frowning.

"Those hijackers sound like real sweethearts."

"I've got to report all this to the police when we get to land," Eric said, rubbing his muscles.

"Sure, lad. We've got a two-way radio on board, but it's out of whack. I was planning to fix it, but didn't get around to it before this whing-ding happened."

"We can phone as soon as we get to the Sheraton-Molokai," Mrs. Harley said. She was clearly the organizer of this team.

"That's where we're going to stay, until we know whether it's safe to go back home. Our house is near the university. We've lived there twenty-eight years." She sighed wistfully.

"Never mind, Susie." Mr Harley stood up. "Everyone in Honolulu is in the same fix now, and at least we're alive. Why, we even got to the right place at the right time and saved another one. It's an ill wind that blows no one some good and all that stuff. Right, my lad?"

Eric started to reply but Mr. Harley went right on talking.

"So I'll get back now to the business of getting us to Molokai. You just hang loose and rest here." In a moment Eric heard the motor start and felt the boat beginning to move.

"You'd better come with us to the Sheraton," Mrs. Harley told Eric. "At least until you can find out about your father and decide what to do. Now you just rest

33

while your clothes are drying. We'll be at Molokai soon.''

Eric lay back on the bunk and closed his eyes again, the food and drink relaxing him. "Thank You, Lord. Thanks loads! You've rescued me again for some reason." He didn't want to impose on these kind people, but, he decided, it would be a good idea to go with them to the hotel. There he could call the police and try to find out what had happened to his dad. He didn't think those hijackers would hurt either his father or the copter pilot once they got to Molokai. On the other hand, they might not have headed for Molokai at all.

Mr. Harley berthed the boat near the sandy Papohaku Beach on Molokai's extreme west coast. The hotel was a huge two-story complex of redwood and ohia wood buildings. The Harleys picked up their reservation and Eric was soon on the phone in their bedroom talking to the Molokai police.

It took a lot of explaining. Eric had to tell his story to several of the law enforcement staff. Finally he learned that no IAF helicopter had landed at either of Molokai's airports. There was no word of his father. The police promised to begin an investigation right away.

Eric was worried. He wondered if he should call Gramps in Washington.

In the living room the Harleys were listening to news reports on the radio. Eric joined them. Some aftershocks continued to be felt, and people were still being evacuated from the Diamond Head area, but the volcano had not yet erupted. When Eric told them about his conversation with the Molokai police, Mr. Harley squinted his green eyes thoughtfully.

"Didn't you say your father was going to do some work here on Molokai?"

"That's right. At the *Puu O Hoku* Ranch."

"Then why not try there? Maybe through some fluke he got there all safe and sound, and neither the airport people nor the police know about it."

Of course! Why hadn't he thought of that? Maybe the copter landed right on the ranch. But when Eric got through to the lodge there, no one had seen his father.

"Dr. Thorne was expected today," the voice on the phone told him, "but has not arrived yet. Would you like to leave a message for him?"

Disappointed, and more worried than ever, Eric left his name and the Harleys' phone number.

"I'm Dr. Thorne's son, Eric. Tell him to call me as soon as he arrives. Tell him I'm safe and that I'm anxious to hear from him."

Mr. Harley's voice was overly hearty when Eric hung up.

"Okay, my lad. Worrying never paid the rent. Chances are everything will work out fine. Now what say you and me and the wife here go find a restaurant and grub down?"

Eric managed a smile. Of course worrying wouldn't help. He knew the Harleys were worried about their home, but they were making the best of things. He would have to do the same, in spite of the sick feeling about his dad.

"Sure, I'd like that," he told them, "but I don't think they'll let me into a restaurant without pants or shoes." Thanks to his dad, he always carried extra money when they were traveling in case they got separated. He was sure he had money enough to take care of his needs for a while. "I'll go see if I can find a store and get some."

He found a shop in the hotel, bought a pair of jeans, a cotton shirt with safari pockets, and some sandals. Over dinner, he discussed with Mr. and Mrs. Harley what he should do.

"Could I spend the night on the boat with the cat?" he asked. "Maybe there'll be news of Dad in the morning."

His rescuers nodded quick approval. Mr. Harley dug into his salad.

"There aren't many people living on Molokai," he said. "Not nearly as big either as the island of Oahu. I don't think the police here will have much trouble finding the helicopter and your father if they're anywhere in this area."

"Have you been on this island before?" Eric asked Mrs. Harley.

"Oh, many times. In fact, Harry and I used to live on a pineapple plantation here when he was overseer, many years ago."

"Did you ever hear of a colony called Eden?"

"Eden!" Mr. Harley roared. Harry was not a quiet man. Several diners in the restaurant turned to look at them curiously. "I've heard of that place. Some mighty strange stories, too. A bunch of weirdos."

Mrs. Harley put her hand on her husband's arm.

"They're just a religious group, Harry. A bunch of Hawaiian teenagers. You see them in the streets in Waikiki, selling flowers to the tourists."

"I meant what I said. They're a bunch of weirdos," Mr. Harley insisted. "They've been in trouble with the police and everyone else on the Islands. What do you want to know about Eden for, lad?"

It seemed wrong to hold back information from these kind people. Eric described his meeting with Noelani at the White House event. But he didn't tell anything about Gramps being the Vice President. Then he went on to describe his meeting with Noelani in the marketplace.

"But she's not weird," Eric assured them, remembering her dark eyes and the scent of ginger in her hair. "She's beautiful. Even writes good poetry, and I usually don't even like poetry."

"And does she talk about Eden in those poetic letters of hers?" Mr. Harley asked him.

"Yeah, she did. She says it's a place where the kids raise their own food, and sort of live off the land. She said they believe in peace and love for each other and the whole world. Stuff like that. It sounded good to me."

Mr. Harley shook his graying head slowly.

"One of those peace-loving kids got himself killed near Eden a while back. I read about it in the papers, but I don't recall the facts. I do know they said there were suspicious circumstances, though." He squinted at Eric. "If this Noelani was my girlfriend, I'd get her out of a place like that."

He spoke with such authority that Eric wondered if Mr. Harley wasn't probably right. Noelani's first letters had described the colony as a wonderful place. The last few letters had not sounded as enthusiastic. And then there was the way she'd been so nervous—almost afraid —in the marketplace, and had told Eric not to try to visit Eden. That was strange.

"But I don't even know where Eden is," he said to the Harleys. "She only said something about it being on the north coast of the island."

"We can get a map from the hotel desk," Mrs. Harley suggested.

The idea activated Eric. He didn't know what had happened to his father, and he didn't know what had happened to Noelani. At least he could get a map and look up Eden. Doing something was better than just sitting and waiting for news.

"I'll go ask at the desk," he said. "Be right back."

Eric brought the map back to their table and they studied it, but no place called Eden could be found. Disappointed, Eric folded it and stuck it in his hip pocket.

After dinner, they walked out to their boat, where Eric was to sleep that night. The magic of Hawaiian evenings returned for a moment. The trade winds were gentle and warm, and the sea shimmered and murmured beside them as they strolled across the sand toward the *Kamalo*.

Mrs. Harley saw it first.

"Look!" she called excitedly. "Over there!"

Eric turned to see. A glow of red across the ocean, in the distance, outlined what must be the crater of Diamond Head. As they watched, they saw a fountain of fire spurt suddenly and burst into an arching shower of brilliant light.

"There it goes!" Mr. Harley muttered sadly.

Eric felt numb and speechless. The sight was frightening and beautiful and unbelievable, all at once, and so he stood staring.

Soon other people from the hotel were swarming out to the beach, all murmuring and exclaiming over the awesome sight of the volcano, forty-odd miles away from them, erupting fiery lava that lighted the night sky. Some were crying. Some sounded angry, and Eric knew they were thinking, like the Harleys, of their homes that might now be destroyed, and wondering if their friends and relatives were safe.

A battery-powered radio near Eric was turned up, and an announcer's voice came clear.

"Diamond Head is erupting. The lava flow appears to be moving in the direction of the ocean. It is believed that the evacuation of the area around the volcano was completed just an hour ago. Rescue units from other islands are now arriving on Oahu.

"Residents are advised to proceed in an orderly fashion to—"

The jabber of fear-filled voices shut out the instructions.

Eric, along with the many others, stayed on the beach with the Harleys watching the spectacle until late that night. When the Harleys returned to their hotel room, Eric boarded the *Kamalo*. He dozed for a little while from sheer exhaustion, then woke with a start. Too many things had happened to him today—his first full day in Hawaii. There was too much on his mind.

Was his father safe? What could have happened to him? Was Noelani still on Oahu, or had she gone back safely to Eden? The man who was watching her—who was he? There was only one thing he was happy about. Alison was safe in Los Angeles. He hoped she wouldn't worry when she got the news. Fortunately Gramps was as close as the telephone.

The *Kamalo* rocked, and the white cat purred beside him in the night, until finally his eyes closed and his thoughts turned into restless, unsettling dreams.

3 • Shipwreck

Early next morning, Eric put on his clothes, ran a comb through his dark hair, fed the cat, and went up on the deck of the *Kamalo*. Across the channel he could barely make out an orange glow in the sky, nothing like the fiery show Diamond Head had put on the night before. But just because the burning lava didn't show up as well in the daylight, he knew it didn't mean the volcano had subsided.

At the hotel, Mr. Harley was already up and waiting. Dressed in bright red pants and a loud shirt that made his large bulk seem even larger, he looked worried.

"There's been no phone call about your father, lad, so we thought you might want to call the police again. See if you can find out what's going on."

But when Eric called, he found there was nothing new. The IAF helicopter hadn't been located, and they were still working on the case, they told him. They would get back to him as soon as they had any word of his father, or anything else to report to him.

"But I can't just stay here and wait," Eric told the Harleys. "I've got to do something myself to try to find Dad."

The older man scratched his head.

"Doesn't seem to be much you can do. But I know how you feel. Let's go get Susie."

Mrs. Harley was working a crossword puzzle in the newspaper. She looked at Eric over the top of her reading glasses. "I've been thinking, Eric, did those two hijackers give you any clue at all as to where they might have been going?"

Eric tried to remember, but he could come up with nothing.

"They only wanted to get off Oahu. That's about all they said."

"Tell us again how they looked."

"One was tall, with dark red hair. The other one was medium height sort of, with brown hair. They were wearing ordinary clothes—you know, dark pants and short-sleeved shirts. But I know their names. They called each other Nat and Jim."

"Hmmm," Mr. Harley said. "Sounds like they were *haoles*."

"What are *haoles*?"

"Oh, the locals—the native islanders—are *kamaainas*. They call Caucasians *haoles*."

Eric thought that a strange name. It sounded like "howlies," and he couldn't figure out the connection. Probably just the Hawaiian word for Caucasian, he decided. While he was thinking this, Mr. Harley was making deductions of his own.

"Probably tourists. Not likely they'd want to spend much time on Molokai. It's a small island. They'd stand out here like warts on a thumb. So maybe they were headed for Maui or the Big Island. Did they have any luggage with them, lad?''

"I don't remember any.''

"Like everyone else, they were leaving Oahu in a big hurry. Maybe they were escaping from more than the volcano.'' Mr. Harley got up from his chair and went to the window to look out at the ocean. "Could be they were running from the police. Did you think of that?''

"You mean criminals? Escaping from the police?''

"Right on, lad. You take my meaning just fine.'' Mr. Harley smiled with satisfaction. "You did give their descriptions to Molokai's finest, didn't you?''

"Oh, sure. I told them everything I could remember.''

"Well, chances are they'll have records on them. These things can be checked. Tourists aren't the only folks attracted to these islands.''

"But it isn't likely they'd let the pilot land in an airport, is it? Not if they were afraid of the police.'' Eric felt frustration at this thought. "They could land anywhere, just about. Anywhere with a clearing big enough for the copter. And that means just about any place on any of the islands.''

The big man turned to Eric and clapped him on the back. "Now, lad, don't let yourself get discouraged. That whirlybird couldn't take them too far, remember, and the police know what they're doing. It might take a few days, but they'll be tracking them down. And since you got the gun away from them, I think your dad and the pilot won't be in too much danger from them.'' He tried to give a cheerful grin, but Eric knew that the Harleys understood the situation just as well as he did.

"Susie, my love,'' Mr. Harley went on. "Will you finish that puzzle and let's go eat? Thinking always gives me an appetite.''

42

It was during breakfast that Eric finally decided what he would do. "I think I'll head for the *Puu O Hoku* Ranch. That's the place I know Dad will go as soon as he can. It's the only meeting place we have."

Mr. Harley agreed that would be a good idea.

"At least that way he'll be able to contact you if he has a chance to."

"He doesn't even know I'm alive," Eric said, fighting back the worry that was never far from the surface. "But there are people at the ranch who were expecting him there yesterday. He'll contact them if he can. I want to be there if he does."

"Sure," Mr. Harley said. "But you're more than welcome to bunk here with us if you've a mind to do that instead. I'm thinking of all the fishing and exploring we could do together if you stayed here!"

"I knew it! He's just wishing you'd stay, Eric, so you two could go off and have a good time and leave me behind with my knitting," Susie Harley teased.

"You don't know how to knit, Susie!"

"Well—my crossword puzzles, then." She smiled at Eric. "But to tell the truth, I enjoy having you around, too."

Eric was touched.

"Any other time, I'd take you up on it."

"Sure enough. We understand." Mr. Harley poured coconut syrup on his pancakes. "But now, how do you plan to get from here to the ranch? It's at the other end of the island, you know. Right smack dab on the east end."

Eric pulled the map out of his pocket and studied it.

"This shows a highway leading past it."

"Fine. But what about a car?"

"Couldn't I rent one?"

"That's going to cost a bundle, lad." Mr. Harley chewed thoughtfully. "Fifteen to twenty dollars a day, and if you stay a few days at the ranch, you can see how that would run up."

Eric checked in his wallet.

"I have enough with me for a couple of days, but my dad will pay for the rest."

"If he turns up at the ranch. You're not sure about that, are you? He might be off somewhere on another island, remember." Susie and Harry glanced at each other as though each could read the other's mind. "Can you handle a boat?" Mr. Harley went on.

"Oh sure. I've taken a sailboat out on the Great Lakes. My dad has a fifty-foot cabin cruiser moored on Lake Michigan."

"Then you can borrow the *Kamalo,* cruise around the north shore, and anchor at Halawa Bay. It's an easy shot from there to the ranch. A bit of a hike, maybe, but at your age that's no sweat. That way you can see the best scenery in the islands as you go."

Eric was surprised at the generous offer and reluctant to accept.

"How can I take your boat? Won't you need it yourselves? And what if I have to keep it a few days while I wait for Dad?"

"We won't be going anywhere until we know what's happened to our house. No, we'll be staying right here, safe and snug," Mrs. Harley said. "Besides, Eric, this way we'll get to see you again when you bring the boat back. Maybe, after your dad comes back, you'll be able to spend a few days here with us then."

Mr. Harley snorted.

"Now why would a handsome young lad want to waste his time with two old coots like us?"

44

His wife smiled wickedly.

"Because I'm going to make friends with every pretty young girl at the hotel. That's why. I'll have them all lined up and waiting for you, Eric."

He laughed with them, but he felt doubtful.

"It's really great of you to offer—but if anything happened to the *Kamalo*, I'd feel awful about it."

They refused to listen to any objections.

"Besides," Mr. Harley said, "you'll have to take Popoki. They won't let us keep her in the hotel, and she's used to the boat. She'll straighten you out if you get off course. That cat's the best sailor since Jacques Cousteau."

Mrs. Harley winked at Eric.

"She's the best sailor since my old man."

There was a rainbow across the horizon as Eric cruised the *Kamalo* through the calm waters along the northern coast of Molokai. Popoki lay on the deck beside him, watching the late morning sunlight glinting on the waves as though she might try to reach out and catch one of the sparkles in her paw. They passed flat, dry fields, patches of scrubby thorn trees, and deserted golden beaches, and Eric thought how strange was the loneliness of this island compared with the crowded beaches of Waikiki. It seemed that here the land had been left almost untouched by civilization.

Eric was a good sailor. He went around a peninsula of flat land and saw the lighthouse at its tip. Here were houses and churches, the green cliffs behind isolating the town from the rest of the island. This must be the settlement of Kalaupapa. Eric had heard about the leper colony that had been formed here, banished from the rest of the world, and about the Belgian priest, Father Damien, who had lived and worked among the sufferers of the dread disease until he, too, had died of it.

"If Dad were here," he said to Popoki, "he would launch into a lecture about sulfone drugs. He'd tell us that leprosy is no longer considered the 'unclean' disease it was in Bible times, and its victims are no longer treated like outcasts." Eric noticed that some patients continued to live here, probably because they had been here so long they had no other homes.

Beyond the peninsula, the coast became wilder. "Feel that, Popoki?" he asked. "The ocean's getting rougher."

There were no more flat stretches of beach, but only towering, folded cliffs, overgrown with verdant rain forests, and waterfalls that dropped thousands of feet into the sea. Overhead, he watched a white bird, delicate and graceful, soar to the tip of a rock. A fairy tern. The pictures he had seen failed to capture the fantastic elegance of that flight.

He passed another waterfall, cascading from the top of a cliff, and saw how the stiff sea wind caught it at the bottom and blew the water back up and out in a dancing swirl, so that it seemed to be falling upside down. A light rain began to fall. Popoki crouched beside his feet so as not to get wet. It was good to have company.

Around the next point of land the rain fell harder and the winds rose, churning the water into white foam as it licked the black rocks just off the shore. Here Eric saw a sea tunnel through the cliff, and watched the water being sucked into its dark maw and come boiling out the other end.

The weather was getting worse.

Eric steered the boat outward, away from the shore. The seas must be twenty feet now, and the wind at least thirty knots. Tops blew off the waves, and scudded foam

along the surface. Standing on the flying bridge, he was soaking wet, finding it difficult to see ahead of him through the mist. Popoki had retired to the shelter of the cabin below.

As the boat lifted to the wave crests and hurtled into the troughs, Eric had to fight the kicking steering wheel. He managed to get around another point of land, only to find islands of rocks looming up at him out of the sea mist. There was no time to steer clear of them. The boat scraped against one of them and tilted to starboard, and Eric had to wedge himself against the bridge and hold tightly to keep from skidding across the wet deck and into the sea.

With a terrible scraping, grinding sound the boat cleared the rock and righted itself, and Eric sighed with relief. It wasn't going to capsize, then! They were safe for the moment, but he'd have to get away from this dangerous shoreline. He tried to steer the *Kamalo* toward the open sea, but the waves were too heavy, splashing over the deck in sheets, rocking the boat shoreward as though it were a toy.

"Can this really be happening to me?" Eric asked himself through clenched teeth. "Fighting the ocean again just twenty-four hours after I was saved from it?"

Suddenly the motor coughed, and was silent. Eric held his breath, hoping the bilge pumps would start again. The engine had taken on too much water, he was sure, but there was no way he could go below to see what he could do. The *Kamalo* was pitching so heavily that if he tried, he'd be washed overboard.

A huge rock island rose out of the mist like the bow of a giant ship and he held his breath, his body shaking, until they had safely passed it. But now there was another, a smaller one. The waves shoved them past that, too, and then, with a lurch, the boat rasped against something and came to a sudden stop.

Jarred off his feet, Eric fell on the slippery deck. For a moment he lay there, wondering what might happen next. When nothing did, he lifted his head, squinted against the pelting rain, and looked at where he had landed.

He was on a shallow strip of black sand on the west side of a deep cove. Looking up, he saw the vertical green cliff that rose far above him, its summit lost in the gray clouds. Ahead was a narrow ledge of fallen boulders that led along the water's edge toward the center of the cove. He got to his feet and, moving carefully on the sloping deck, he went back to check the engine. When he lifted off the cover, he saw that it was, indeed, waterlogged, and the bottom of the boat was filled with sea water. He could bail it out, but the engine might have more damage than he could repair. He'd better not mess with it, and maybe make it worse. The best thing to do would be to look for a town or village near here and get a mechanic to do it.

The *Kamalo* was tilted to starboard, but Eric didn't want to leave the boat without anchoring it. The same waves that had driven it here might well loosen it and drag it back into the ocean. Working the winch by hand he lowered the anchor to the beach, then secured its chain around a large rock. That done, he went down to the cabin.

Popoki was huddled on the bunk, her almond-shaped eyes shining in the dim light. Eric comforted her a little, then opened the chest and took out the sandwiches Mrs. Harley had left for him. Popoki ate the little pieces of flaked tuna greedily.

"You're not that scared, then," Eric told her, "or you

wouldn't have an appetite. Now do I leave you here, or take you with me?" He wished he'd been able to leave the animal with the Harleys, but suggesting that might have seemed ungrateful.

Now—how to get out of this cove and up that steep cliffside was the real problem facing Eric. Even if he did find his way to the *Puu O Hoku* Ranch, he wasn't sure when he could get back to the *Kamalo* with help to start the motor and return it to the Harleys.

"Here's the problem," he told Popoki. "If I leave you here, you might starve. Or be killed by marauding animals. Or even drown in the surf. If I take you with me, the situation might be very similar!" So he sat on the bunk and finished off the sandwiches as he tried to decide what to do.

The rain was subsiding now. The winds had died down, and it was the time to push on.

Eric looked around the small boat's cabin to see what he might take with him that would be useful. He found a flashlight and a jackknife in a drawer, decided against carrying any of the fishing poles, but took some fishing hooks and line that he found in a small plastic box. If he needed to fish for his dinner, he could use pebbles as sinkers and a branch for a pole. And he would take that butane lighter, too. He'd need a fire to cook the fish, after all. He put the lighter, the box, and the jackknife in the pockets of his jeans and hung the flashlight on his belt.

"That might be very useful," he said to himself as he noticed a coiled length of nylon rope in the drawer. But the coil wouldn't fit in his pocket. Fine, then he'd wind it around his waist, under his shirt. He was going to have to climb up the cliff and find the main road. Some rope might make that climb a lot safer.

He turned to look at the cat.

"Okay, I'm ready to go now, so it's up to you. You want to come with me, or stay here?"

Popoki yawned and stretched, then settled down with folded paws and gazed at him with inscrutable eyes.

"Okay." Eric was almost disappointed. "I'll prop the cabin door open for you. You'll need to get out and hunt your own food until I get back." He poured water from the sink into the cat's bowl. "Hope the water holds out, otherwise you'll have to hunt that, too."

Popoki merely blinked.

Eric went up the cabin stairs into the sudden sunlight. Along the shore the sea was murky, but on the horizon, it melted into the blue sky. Only a few dark clouds in the west gave any sign that there had ever been a storm.

"It must be two o'clock," Eric estimated, squinting toward the sun. "Surely I can get out of this place before dark."

He strode across the short stretch of beach and then up onto the rocky, crumbling ledge where he had to tread carefully over the rounded boulders and around the places where the shelf had almost eroded away. The ledge sloped upward, and as he climbed, it became a slippery, muddy trail through the dark green foliage, angling up along the cliff. He moved carefully, wishing he had bought tennis shoes instead of these sandals. The leather soles slid on the soaked ground. He took them off and went barefoot, gripping the slimy mud with his toes.

A misstep here would mean a drop of fifty feet or more to the jagged rocks.

The sound of the pounding surf became less as he climbed higher. Now he could hear gurgling water. He looked around and saw a stream tumbling out of the hillside, splashing down to the black rim of the bay.

51

Good, Popoki would have fresh water. Eric hoped that when he needed some himself, there would be more of these streams along the cliffs.

But where was this trail leading? It had to lead somewhere. From time to time the path disappeared under creeping vegetation, but Eric pushed the vines aside until he found it again. A trail meant someone had come this way. He had to follow it. It was the only sign of human life in this place.

By this time the cliffs around him were hiding the sun, so that he seemed to walk through a green cave that smelled of decayed logs, moss, and rotting fruit. Now and then a patch of ginger blossoms wafted their scent toward him, and he stopped to breathe in the perfume and remember Noelani before he trudged onward.

Something rustled in the bushes behind him. He stopped and turned his head to look, but there was nothing there. Funny, he could have sworn someone was following him! As he walked on he heard it again. There was no mistaking the sound of movement in the underbrush.

Someone was behind him!

He stopped and turned again, but he could see nothing, and the noise stopped at the same time he did. He was getting spooked here in this gloomy rain forest, all alone. Who could know what might be lurking in this dense, wild place? Nervously he waited, but heard no more sounds. So he turned and went on, the hairs at the back of his neck prickling. One step—two—three—and there was that sound again! Eric stopped, and this time the noise continued for a fraction of a second after. He whirled, and faced the stalker.

"Popoki!"

The big white cat stood in a patch of fern beside the

trail, one paw lifted, looking at him.

Eric laughed, relief flooding through him.

"Dumb cat!" he chuckled. Popoki, recognizing it as a truce, came to him and rubbed against his leg. "So you decided to come with me after all?"

Popoki sat down and gazed past him, looking unconcerned.

Grinning, Eric turned to follow the trail again. Of course the cat wouldn't walk beside him. Cats were stalkers, not companions. Still, it eased the loneliness of his plight in some small way.

After nearly an hour, Eric found himself at what he judged to be the center of a bay-like area, and approaching a clearing in the rain forest.

"What a sight!" he breathed, wishing Alison were here with her camera to capture the beauty around him. Something white glinted through the greenery ahead. A house? Unbelievingly, he ran the last few feet through a pandanus grove and emerged onto an open plateau.

The steep, folded cliffs ringed it in, and below it, a gradual slope led down toward the rocky shore, where Eric could see two boats bobbing on the swell. Here was a collection of poorly-made shacks, some of them painted white, some brown and weather stained, and all of them dilapidated. A few fishing nets and poles leaned against some of them; a ring of blackened stones surrounded a large cooking pit in the middle of the clearing, and lines stretched between the trees behind the shacks bore articles of clothing left to dry. The whole place looked deserted.

But Eric was jubilant. He had found his fishing village, or whatever this was. There had to be people here somewhere.

Raising his voice, Eric called out "Hello! Anybody

here?'' His words echoed from side to side between the surrounding cliffs, resounding in the stillness.

He waited a moment, listening for an answer, but there was none. He called again and walked up to the nearest hut, a crudely-fashioned building of wood thatched with grass and palm fronds. Segments of bamboo on strings hung across the opening, serving as a curtain.

"Hello! Anyone in here?"

Eric drew back the crudely-fashioned bamboo curtain to look inside. All he could see in the dim interior was a couch, a heap of clothing on the dirt floor, some pillows scattered around. There seemed to be no one inside. He let the curtain drop and turned away. Where was everyone? Had he come all the way up that dangerous trail only to find some kind of Hawaiian ghost town?

He ran toward another hut, shouting his question through the stillness, but the only answer was the squawk of a bird in the rain forest. An eerie feeling made him shiver and he glanced behind to see if his companion, Popoki, was still with him, just in time to see the end of her tail disappear around the side of the shack. Probably chasing a mouse or a rat, he decided.

Past a broken fence around what seemed to be the start of a vegetable garden, Eric passed more run-down shacks. On an ancient couch sagging in the shade of a blossoming plumeria tree, he sat on the worn cushions to rest and put on his sandals. The silence was almost painful as he got up and moved slowly toward another hut that stood apart from the others, a short distance away.

A twig snapped behind him. He whirled, to see a shadow melt into the shade of a clump of bushes a few feet away. Popoki again? No, that shadow was too big for a cat. It was big enough to be the shadow of a man. But of course there was no one there. "I'm getting jumpy, that's all," he assured himself.

First Popoki had given him a scare, and now he was ready to imagine anything. Still, why was there no one around? Surely someone must live in these shacks. But who? Maybe they weren't too friendly. Maybe they were following him with weapons, ready to kill him.

Oh come on, Eric, he told himself. Your imagination is getting the best of you! His throat was dry with nervousness. He couldn't stay here any longer. He wanted to get out of this place. It was empty and strange, and there was something wrong. He turned to go back across the clearing.

Just then someone moved behind him.

Before he could see who it was, his arms had been grabbed and pinned behind his back. He struggled fiercely to get away, but whoever it was held him in a painfully strong grip.

4 • *The Gods of Eden*

"Who are you?" a male voice growled in his ear. "What are you doing here?"

"Let me go!" Eric twisted and pulled with all his strength.

"Hey, Kimo!" the man who held him called. "I got him! Hurry! He strong one!"

Eric heard running footsteps and saw a tall, black-haired youth crash through the bushes. Brown-skinned, he was bare except for a pair of faded denim shorts. The Hawaiian glared at Eric.

"What you want here, *haole*?"

Eric stopped his struggles, took a deep breath, and tried to stay calm.

"My boat was beached down in the entrance to the cove. I'm looking for someone to help me start it, or tell me how to get to a main road."

Kimo studied him under thick black eyebrows.

"You alone?"

"Sure I'm alone."

"Okay, Aleka. Let him loose. He not go nowhere."

Eric rubbed his wrists as his captor released him. They stared at Eric. Just as curious, Eric stared back.

Both Kimo and Aleka seemed to be about his age, sixteen or seventeen perhaps, and both were dressed the same way. Aleka was shorter than his companion but just as muscular. Both of them looked angry, suspicious, and not in the least frightened. They bore little resemblance to the friendly Hawaiian males on the travel posters.

"Just tell me how to get to the main road," Eric said. "I'm lost."

"Lost?"

Kimo didn't seem to believe him.

"Right. I'm looking for the *Puu O Hoku* Ranch."

The two Hawaiians exchanged glances.

"No main road here. No ranch," Kimo said.

"Yeah," Aleka added. "We take you where you really going."

He grabbed Eric's arm, and Kimo moved to his other side to do the same.

"Where are you taking me?" Eric gasped as they dragged him across the clearing.

But they ignored him, forcing him along between the two of them.

Eric had no choice but to go with them. Struggling was useless. But he wondered what kind of place he had stumbled into. Whatever it was, he didn't think he was going to like it.

Silently, the two men forced Eric up a slope and through a grove of koa and cypress trees. Now, for the first time, he could see a large building standing on the crest of the hill. It was a big frame house, more solidly built than the huts below, painted white with a narrow porch and an arched green door. Eric was pushed up the steps, and Kimo knocked at the door.

It was opened by a young girl, about thirteen, her long, dark hair decorated with a ring of purple blossoms. She stared at Eric curiously and twisted the fabric of her ragged white blouse with nervous fingers.

"Who's he?"

Kimo spoke brusquely.

"We bring him to Pele."

"She's in garden. They all there. Work time."

Kimo pushed past the girl and beckoned Aleka to bring Eric inside. "Go get her. Tell her we got stranger."

The girl hesitated only a moment, still staring at Eric. Then she darted off toward the back of the house.

Eric looked around. He was in a large, bright room with grass mats on the floor and Hawaiian tapa cloth covering the couch and chairs. One wall was made up entirely of shelves, crowded with paperback books and magazines. A two-way radio was set up in a corner, on a wooden desk. The walls and low tables were decorated with carved wooden statues of ancient Hawaiian gods and goddesses. Eric had an uncomfortable feeling they were more than decorations.

He was not invited to sit down, but stood with his two guards at one of the big windows that looked down through the screen of trees to the shacks below. He wondered who it was they'd sent for. Pele? That was the name of the legendary goddess who punished her people by causing volcanoes to erupt—the name the old Hawaiian mentioned in the marketplace. Well, he wasn't afraid of legends.

The large woman who swept in through a door at the end of the room was imposing. Tall, with white hair piled high on her head and held with a shell comb, she had a face as fierce as those of any of the carved figures. Her dress was long and full, the color of orchids, and she wore many necklaces, bracelets, and rings of shell and gold and coral. But it was her eyes that were her most impressive feature. Dark brown and widely spaced, they seemed to take in every detail of Eric's appearance in one brief glance, then pierce under his flesh to seek out his heart. She sat down in a nearby chair and stared at him silently for a moment.

"Where did you find him?" she asked Kimo.

"Poking around in houses down there."

Kimo jerked his head toward the huts.

"He's alone?"

Her voice was low and harsh.

"We didn't see no one else."

The woman spoke now to Eric.

"Who are you?"

"My name's Eric Thorne. I wasn't poking around, I was trying to find someone to give me directions. My boat had engine trouble and got washed ashore near here. I need help to—"

"Eric Thorne?" The big woman rose out of her chair.

"Yes I know you," she said after she studied him closely. She turned, went to the shelves, and removed a thick folder. Then she rummaged through it and pulled out a clipping from a magazine, holding it up beside his face. "Here. This is you. I know you." She waved the clipping triumphantly.

Eric couldn't believe his eyes. It was the article from *Faces* magazine, and there was his picture. Maybe she would believe him now.

"Yes," he said, relieved. "That's my picture."

Maybe now they would believe he was a visitor here in

the islands, that he wouldn't know his way around.

But Pele didn't look any friendlier.

"How many others are with you? Where are they hiding?"

Eric was confused.

"There's nobody with me. I told you, I'm alone. I'm lost. My boat—"

"What has she told you?" Pele thundered.

"Who? What are you talking about? I don't understand."

The woman glared at him, her eyes glinting with anger, her face ugly with fury.

"You were seen with her. In the marketplace, on Oahu. She told you lies then, and in her letters to you."

Something exploded in Eric's brain.

"Noelani? You mean Noelani? Then this must be Eden!"

"You lie, Eric Thorne! It's no use pretending you did not come here because of Noelani, because of the lies she told you. You have come to Eden to try to destroy us."

Eric felt helpless under her barrage of accusations. How could he convince her he was telling the truth? He didn't even understand what she was talking about.

"Noelani hasn't told me anything. Ask her. She'll tell you. And I certainly didn't come here to destroy you or anyone else. I didn't even know where I was!"

But Pele ignored him and spoke to the two men.

"Go. Take Kala and Pekelo with you. Search the colony. Find whoever is with him and bring them here. Awiwi!"

Kimo and Aleka went swiftly out the door. Pele watched them go, then strode to a chair and dropped the folder and the clipping onto it. Turning back to Eric, she folded her arms regally and spoke with venomous anger.

60

"That Noelani. She is a *kauwa*, an outcast among us. She does not deserve to be one of the chosen."

Eric felt suddenly protective.

"Noelani has told me good things about Eden. I don't know why you're so angry with her."

This was true. Noelani had said nothing bad about her life here, although Eric had a feeling she had not been telling him the whole story. But Noelani had certainly never mentioned this woman. That was strange, because this person who called herself Pele was obviously important in Eden. She was the head honcho of the whole place, judging from her manner.

"Why don't you ask Noelani to come here and tell you herself?" He went on. "Where is she?"

Pele only watched him with cold eyes.

Eric tried again.

"I didn't see her after that quake on Oahu yesterday. Did she get back here okay?"

"So! I am right. You did come here to find her. But you should be worried about yourself, Eric Thorne. The Children of Eden do not welcome their enemies!"

She turned her back on him and faced the carvings. She threw back her head, closed her eyes, and seemed to be chanting to herself, or to some unseen presence. Part of what she said was in the Hawaiian language, but one part was in English.

"We have power over the fires in the earth's center, in the cleansing waters, and in the fire that streaks from the sky." The husky chanting voice chilled him.

Her chant ended, she turned her penetrating eyes upon him again.

"Eric Thorne, you will be sorry you ever came here."

Eric tried to keep his voice calm and reasonable. This woman was intimidating, but he must not let her sense

61

that he was fearful of what she had in mind.

"I didn't come to this place on purpose. I told you that," Eric insisted. "I've tried to explain how it happened. Go down and see my beached boat for yourself. I'd never have run it into all those rocks on purpose."

Her only answer was an icy stare.

Where was Noelani? What kind of an evil place was this, Eric wondered. What did Pele think Noelani had told him?

There was a noise of footsteps outside, then a knock, and at Pele's bidding, Kimo and Aleka came in. Kimo carried a pair of binoculars.

"We find no one," he told Pele. "Not down below, not anywhere around. But we saw this one's boat. Like he say, it up on beach on rocks." Kimo handed the woman his binoculars. "You see it from up farther."

Pele took the binoculars and went out, striding across the porch. Eric and the others waited silently until she came back. She handed Kimo the glasses and turned to gaze thoughtfully at Eric.

"So! You're very stupid. Maybe very cunning?" Then she spoke to the two others. "Bring him to the garden."

She turned and left the room through the door she had entered earlier.

Her threatening manner angered Eric. He wasn't afraid of her, but her suspicious attitude made him more curious than ever to see Noelani. She'd be able to tell him what was going on. And when he left here, he'd try to get her to go with him. He didn't like this Pele or her two bodyguards one little bit. Weirdos, Mr. Harley had called them. Eric was beginning to agree.

When Kimo and Aleka made a move toward him, he drew away.

62

"Keep your hands off me. I'm going."

He followed the big woman, with the others close behind him.

The doorway led into a hall with a musty odor that ran the length of the building. At its end was another door that led out to a lanai. As Eric emerged, he saw why the huts had been deserted. Everyone in Eden must be gathered here.

A crowd of girls sat on an expanse of tree-shaded grass, weaving flowers into garlands. It should have been a happy scene, but something felt terribly wrong. Leis, Eric thought, like those he had seen Noelani selling in the marketplace. Beyond them, a group of young men were busy weaving fishing nets. He guessed there must be fifty or sixty of these Hawaiian teenagers altogether, and all of them seemed too thin and too quiet. Their clothing was ragged. Their faces were sad, empty. His eyes searched for Noelani among the girls, but she was not there.

As Eric and his guards followed Pele out of the house, the group looked up from their work and stared at him curiously. Eric smiled but they seemed afraid to respond. Did they, too, believe he was an enemy?

Pele strode to one end of the lanai, and Eric saw that the wall behind her had been painted with a mural of vivid colors, showing a live volcano erupting fire and a white-haired woman standing on the edge of the caldera, her hands raised triumphantly. It was Pele, the volcano goddess. The face on the mural was the face of the woman standing in front of it, the same fierce face and magnetic eyes.

Pele spoke into a microphone. It seemed oddly out of place and quite unnecessary, but it heightened the drama as her voice resounded through the tropical landscape.

"Children of Eden, we have a stranger in our garden." She paused, until everyone stopped working and crowded into the lanai.

"His name is Eric Thorne. He came from the mainland, drawn here by the poisoned words of a snake who lived among us; she who tried to betray us. His heart is turned against us. He came here alone to spy on us, but was found out. If we let him return to his friends, they will come back here and destroy Eden."

As she talked, Eric lost some of his nerve. He felt his throat going dry and his heart pounding. What was this woman planning to do—keep him here by force? He couldn't believe this was happening in part of the United States of America. To civilized people. Or were they civilized? Maybe living here on this wild, isolated coast had made them revert to some primitive ways.

But Noelani had told him this was a religious colony, and its name was certainly Biblical! Still, she hadn't ever explained what she meant by "religious." Judging by the carved gods in the house, the mural on the wall, and the tall wooden statues he could see around the edge of the garden, whatever the religion was it was certainly not Christian! Something strangely pagan and evil. He remembered that the ancient Hawaiian gods advocated war and human sacrifice. But all that had died out hundreds of years ago, hadn't it?

He wanted to believe that.

Somehow, here in this quiet valley with the folded cliffs towering over them, hiding the sun, and the rain forest pressing in against them, he could believe the old ways might still have some followers. He shivered and tried to think of something to say, something to do, but nothing came to him.

There were murmurs of surprise, even anger, as Pele

announced what she had decided was the reason for Eric's arrival in Eden. Eric could feel the group's hostility growing as Pele went on.

"If we let him go, the evil ones with their guns and sirens will come here to take you all away!"

The muttering of the crowd grew louder. "No." "Don't let him go!"

Eric felt a chill as Pele's voice rose.

"If he leaves here, you will be destroyed along with all the rest of them! You will be lost in the evil madness of the world, and you will die with the others in it."

The crowd moved closer to Eric, shouting its disapproval, until a line of grim-faced young Hawaiians stood only four or five feet away from him.

Pele raised her arms and her excited voice once more resembled a chant.

"Then what will we do with him, Children of Eden? Do we let him go back to bring evil upon us?"

"No!" It was a unanimous chorus that echoed across the rocky hillside. "No! No!"

Pele knew exactly when to spread her arms for silence. She spoke more quietly now.

"But we can't keep him here. He cannot live with the chosen of Eden. He is a *haole*. He carries the sins of his world. He cannot be allowed to live through the holocaust and infect our world once again!"

The eyes of the angry crowd stared at him. Eric tried to make sense of Pele's words. This woman was working her followers into a frenzy of hatred and fear. She sounded quite insane to him.

Sensing a mounting fear within him, Eric shouted so all could hear him. "Hey, listen to me. This is all crazy! I haven't done anything except come here by accident. I don't know what you're talking about—evil and holocausts and all that stuff. I'm certainly not here to spy on you! I don't have any friends waiting to come here! I'm all alone, and I got lost. Just tell me how to get out of here and I will. You'll never see me or hear from me again.''

Pele's smile was ugly.

"There are snakes in Eden," she said to the crowd, "hissing poisoned words to hide their black hearts."

"I didn't even know this was Eden!" Eric shouted desperately. "It isn't on the map."

Pele shook her head.

"He lies. It is easy to lie. But I can show you the truth.''

She beckoned to a girl near her and whispered something in her ear. The girl ran into the house.

Now someone spoke up from the crowd.

"Why we not let him go? He have one hard time finding a way through rain forest. He could die trying."

The person who spoke moved to the front of the group, and Eric saw he was stocky, well-built, and handsome. He wore a faded pair of blue jeans. His face was broad, blunt-featured but striking.

Pele regarded the speaker with disdain.

"Listen better, Kala. I said he has others waiting to come here to take us away. If he leaves here, he will find a way to reach his friends."

Kala stood there grinning, saying nothing more, but Eric felt a surge of gratitude. At least somebody in this crowd wanted to let him go.

The girl came back, and Eric saw her hand some papers to Pele. That clipping! The one from *Faces* magazine! And now Pele was holding it up in front of the throng.

"Look. Now you can see how this Eric Thorne lies. I

66

found this in the hut of the other snake among us—
Noelani the *kauwa*. She wrote him letters, and he wrote
back to her, and they met together to plot against us.''

She held the magazine clipping so that everyone could
see Eric's face on it.

He tried to protest, but Pele drowned out his words
with her own.

"What will we do with him?" she thundered at her
followers, and Eric heard, with horror, the words someone in the crowd shouted back at her:

"Sacrifice him! *Kapu wela!*"

Pele smiled cruelly.

"The burning taboo. Punishment by fire."

She looked at Eric with a strange light in her eyes.

"You're insane!" he growled in disbelief at what he
had heard. The words were out of his mouth before he
could stop them.

Her smile only grew more determined.

"Pele will have her sacrifice!" she said in a voice so
low that only Eric and the few people close to her could
hear. It was more emphatic to Eric than any shout.

A girl near the front of the crowd began to cry, and
several others showed signs of distress.

Kala moved a few steps forward and spoke to Pele.

"If he got friends, Pele, won't they come here to look
for him? Won't they find out? Why not turn him loose in
forest, or put him out to sea? Why not let wild pigs or
sharks get him?"

"Stupid!" Pele glared at him. "In the fire, nobody
will find his bones." She turned from him and spoke
again into the microphone. "So," she said threatening-
ly, "not all of you agree to the *kapu wela*?"

She looked at them so ferociously that they all fell
silent again.

Something small and white moved around the corner of the house. It was Popoki. The cat went to Pele's feet and looked up at her. The woman was still glaring at the crowd. Popoki passed from Pele to Kala and then moved on in Eric's direction. A patch of grass at the edge of the lanai caught her attention and she wandered to it, sniffed, then backed away, frightened.

Several of the younger girls giggled nervously and pointed to the cat. Pele looked to see what it was. Her eyes widened, and she opened her mouth as though to say something. She seemed to think better of it and waited, watching the cat.

Eric watched the cat numbly as she paused to sniff at Kimo's feet, then looked up and saw Eric. She came right to him then, meowing. Tail up, back arched, she rubbed against his leg in greeting.

Pele laughed in triumph.

"This cat does not belong here. The gods are giving us a sign. They have sent a wild creature from the forest to confirm what must be done. Does any one of you still doubt?"

Eric stared at her in disbelief. "The cat came here with me," he said, but his words were lost in the noise. There were gasps and shouts, and he could tell that everyone there believed what Pele said. Pele had won. Kimo and Aleka grabbed his arms and held him in a painful grasp.

Pele pointed at him.

"You will be sacrificed to the fire, tomorrow, at dawn!"

5 • *Overnight Guest in Eden*

The shed had no windows. Eric felt as though he had been lying on the floor and smelling the sour odor of the place for hours.

His head ached, his back was sore, and the rawhide strips binding his wrists and ankles bit painfully into his flesh. Close to panic, he talked to himself and to the Lord.

"Lie still, Eric," he began. "Save your energy for your escape—"

"Lord, this is wild! This sure enough is Satan's territory. Right here on this beautiful island You have created, too! I'm in another tight spot. Help me know what to do—and how I can get these kids out of this evil woman's grip. Especially, help me find Noelani."

Over and over he found his mind turning to plans for escape—talking about his ideas in prayer—his father's whereabouts—back to prayer for God's protection in this satanic place.

There was no way he was going to be thrown into that

fire pit Aleka and Kimo had shown him. The deep hole in the earth reminded him of the crater of a volcano. Surrounding it were grimacing statues, and standing guard beyond them was an outer rim of gray barked kukui trees, the sacred trees of the ancient Hawaiians.

Working his body over to get some fresh air through the crack under the door, Eric struggled to think clearly.

Without God's help all the odds were on Pele's side. One thought kept returning:

"Why did God let all these things happen to me—all since I came to the Islands this week?

"God didn't let this happen to you," Eric heard his own voice. "You did. Two days ago God had the Harleys scoop you out of the ocean, and today you walked right into this jungle mantrap. If I were you, I'd be too embarrassed to ask God for help again. What do you think God operates, some kind of celestial swat team just for your benefit?"

Was there any truth in those words? They sounded like something Alison would have said. "Eric, you're disaster prone!" she had said many times. "You're an accident going somewhere to happen!"

If he ever got out of here he would be willing to admit she had a point.

Alison's scoldings were usually followed by a dose of truth and common sense from Aunt Rose. Dear Aunt Rose! Just last week she'd instructed Eric.

"You can't ask for God's help too often, Eric Thorne, in fact, *you* should probably pray more often—especially for good sense to keep you out of the scrapes into which you seem to gravitate. So keep praying—and be ready to face whatever comes, with courage and with the Lord's help!"

Eric thought he was beginning to hear the first sounds

of morning when he remembered the jackknife he had taken from the *Kamalo*. He rolled over and felt the hard shape in his jeans pocket. After what seemed like an eternity of trying, he knew he could not get it out.

"Wish I'd never remembered it," he murmured into the darkness.

After a while he heard a scraping noise like metal against metal. Someone was trying to get in! Sweat broke out on his forehead and his heart pounded.

"They couldn't be coming after me!" he groaned. "Not yet—"

The noise went on, small and furtive. He was afraid to call out. He could only lie there and listen. Now there was another noise, the slight groaning of the hinges as the door opened slowly, and Eric could see a strip of lighter gray in the darkness of the shed. A silhouette moved against that strip and he heard someone coming inside.

"Who's there?" he whispered in panic.

"Shhhhh!" Whoever it was moved softly toward him. "You wanna get out of here, don't you?"

The voice sounded familiar, but he couldn't put a face with it.

"Sure," he said quietly.

Could it be that someone was willing to risk helping him escape? A figure bent over him. He could feel hands working around his ankles. Suddenly his feet were free. He moved them, feeling the pains shooting through them as he struggled to sit up.

"Who are you?"

He peered into the darkness.

"Kala. Shhh! They all asleep. Here. Hold out wrists. I'll cut ties."

Gratefully, Eric held his wrists back in the direction of

71

the voice, and felt Kala's fingers take hold of them and the pressure of a knife slicing through the ties. Now his hands were free, and he shook his sore wrists to get circulation through them. Then he got to his feet, swaying, grabbing at a nearby carton to steady himself.

"Come on," Kala whispered, heading for the door.

Eric forced his numb feet to walk until he had slipped through the crack in the doorway and was following Kala outside.

A pale moon, partly covered by clouds, shed enough light for him to see his rescuer ahead of him, disappearing into a dark patch of forest. And he saw something else. A small, white shape ran out of the shadows and brushed against him with a little cry. He reached down and picked up the cat, then hurried after Kala.

The Hawaiian seemed to move silently as he sped along a path through the rain forest, and Eric felt clumsy as his sandals knocked against stones and fallen branches. Each sound was like a shock wave that might reach Pele's ears. Popoki meowed and struggled to get out of his arms. He let her go and saw her scurry ahead, then dive into the underbrush.

Eric found it hard to keep up with Kala, who raced ahead, sure-footed, but he managed to keep him in sight by the moon's faint light.

They started going downhill, and suddenly Eric saw Pele's house through the trees. They had circled up and around behind it, and now they were going past it! Kala must be heading for the shore. Eric didn't understand, but all he could do was follow. Still, he wished they'd gone the other way, up the cliff. As forbidding and impassable as it seemed, he preferred that to coming this close to Pele and the Children of Eden again.

The path was muddy. His sandals slid on it. He wished

he could take them off, but if he stopped to do that, he might lose sight of Kala. The very thought made him break into a run until he was right behind the muscular Hawaiian racing down the slope.

Suddenly he heard voices. A man and a woman, laughing, sounding very close. He paused and looked around, his heart pounding, but Kala paid no attention. Eric ran after him, hoping they hadn't heard the beating of his heart and the slapping of his shoes. There was no way to tell. The voices stopped, and he couldn't hear anyone coming after them. Not yet.

Now he smelled the sharp salt scent of the sea and heard the waves breaking, and he remembered something. Kala was the one who had asked Pele to release Eric.

"Leave him to the sharks—" Wasn't that what he'd said? Well, that was okay. Eric could swim. The main thing was to get away from Eden, wasn't it? Could sharks be any worse? But he wondered if he could trust Kala. Why had he freed him from that shed?

There was no time to wonder. It took all Eric's strength now to keep up with his guide running just ahead of him. And to navigate around and over the boulders was becoming increasingly difficult. Ahead, he could see the trees thinning and moonlight shimmering on the water. They were coming to the beach.

But it wasn't really a beach. It was a stretch of large, sea-sprayed rocks edging the sea. Eric scrambled over them, bruising his elbows and knees as he slipped on the wet stones. There was no time to step carefully from rock to rock. He jumped from one to the next and hoped for the best. At last he stood beside Kala at the water's edge and tried to catch his breath.

The Hawaiian was looking at the ocean, at the waves

that swelled high as they came toward them, then ebbed with a grinding, pounding sound that Eric realized must be caused by rocks rolling back and forth under the water.

"High tide," Kala muttered.

"What are we going to do?"

"You can swim?"

"Swim?" Eric was surprised. "Swim where?"

"Around there," Kala pointed out toward the neck of the cove.

They stood at the center of the U-shaped inlet, with the colony of Eden on the slopes behind them. To their right, a rocky cliff rose high and sheer. Kala was indicating a ledge of rocks at one end of the U. Directly across from where he pointed, perhaps a mile to the west, was the beach where the *Kamalo* was anchored.

Eric looked at the angry sea. He had no desire to spend more time in the open ocean without a boat.

"You going to leave me to the sharks after all?" he asked.

Kala's teeth gleamed in the darkness as he laughed.

"How about if I climbed up that cliff? Couldn't I get away from here that way?"

Even as he asked, Eric knew that was probably impossible. The rock wall rose straight up into the sky, with scattered ledges that only a mountain goat could navigate.

"Come on."

Kala moved toward the pounding surf and stood for a moment while foam covered his legs, before he dived into a wave.

Eric watched him, surprised. Kala was going to make the swim with him! He pulled off his sandals and hesitated, reluctant to dive in among those grinding rocks he could hear, but knowing that he had to. A meowing behind him made him turn to see the white cat scrambling across the rocks.

"Popoki! Don't try to follow me!"

He took a deep breath and plunged into a breaking wave.

The rolling rocks gouged against his legs and ankles pushing him back toward shore. He got to his feet and crouched, waiting for another breaker. As it came, he dived into it and fought to stay under the water, swimming as hard as he could, waiting until he was forced to come up for air. And this time it was all right. He'd made it! He was beyond the surf. He could see Kala just ahead of him, swimming parallel to the cliff, and the going was easier now. Eric swam rhythmically, trying to keep his breathing even and his thoughts calm.

How far could it be to the mouth of the cove? Half a mile, maybe? And as long as there was moonlight, he could keep Kala, and the white surge of the sea against the cliff, in sight. The Hawaiian was an expert swimmer, and he must know these waters and terrain pretty well. He must be leading Eric somewhere to safety. It was too bad about leaving the Harleys' cat and their boat behind, but he'd come back with help to fix the *Kamalo*, and he'd look for Popoki, too. As long as she didn't try to swim after him, she'd probably be okay for a few days. Did cats swim? Some of them did, he was sure, but no cat would ever make it past those breakers.

Thinking about the cat must be making him imagine things. When he turned his head to take a breath, he thought he saw a small, white animal running along the side of the cliff above him. But of course there were mountain goats on the island. He'd seen some just after they passed Kalapaupau yesterday. Two of them, standing

75

on a crag. Had that been only yesterday? It seemed like weeks ago.

A swell made him break the rhythm of his crawl stroke and he took in a mouthful of salt water. He spit it out quickly and picked up the six-beat movements of his arms and legs, his thoughts going back to his problems again. He'd have to find out about Dad as soon as he could and call Alison in Los Angeles. News of the volcano must have reached her by this time.

And Noelani. He'd never found out where she was. He didn't like to think that Pele had done her any harm. If he ever came back here for the *Kamalo* and Popoki, he'd bring the police with him. They'd want to talk to Pele after he told them she'd planned to make him a human sacrifice. Surely she hadn't done that to Noelani!

He lifted his head to look for Kala, and there just ahead, he saw the end of the point. Kala was heading in toward it. A lava ledge jutted low over the water, and he swam in closer, seeing Kala grasp the ledge and scramble up on it. A few more strokes and Eric was pulling himself out of the water.

For a moment both of them lay stretched out on the ledge, panting, while the sea grasped at them, fingers of foam clawing at the rocks. As soon as Eric caught his breath again, he sat up.

"Well, we're here. Now what?"

"We got away from Eden," Kala said, not moving. "Hang loose now. They not come after us."

"How do you know?" Eric squinted back along the line of the cliff to the darkness that was Eden. "They've got boats. I saw them. How do you know they won't be after us?"

"They all asleep now. They not know we gone until morning. By then it too late."

"But we can't stay here!"

"We stay here and rest. Then we move on."

Kala sounded sleepy.

"Where are we going?"

"Just around point."

Kala refused to say more, and in a few minutes his breathing grew heavy and regular, and Eric knew he had fallen asleep. He wondered how Kala could relax enough to sleep on this rocky ground, soaking wet from the swim and the sea mist that sprayed them, but when he lay back himself and closed his eyes he, too, fell into a deep, exhausted sleep.

He was awakened by something smelly and wet rubbing against his cheek. He opened his eyes; and in the gray light he looked into Popoki's yellow ones.

"How did you get here?" he said, surprised and happy to see her. "Was that you running along the cliff?"

Still drowsy, he pushed her away and closed his eyes to sleep again, but the cat curled up against his chest and settled there, purring. It was nearly dawn.

That's strange, Eric thought sleepily. He couldn't *feel* the purr against his body, but he could *hear* it.

He sat up, his heart jumping. Cats don't purr that loud! It was the sound of a motor in the distance. One of the boats from Eden? He slapped at Kala's shoulder.

"Wake up!"

"What?" Kala's eyes popped open.

"They're coming after us."

Eric got up, and picked up the cat.

Kala rose in one swift movement, and stood listening for a second. He squinted at the western horizon, then turned and went quickly over the rocks and around the point, Eric following. Here the lava ledge broadened into a grotto sculptured by the sea, with tiny islands and cavelike niches. Kala seemed to know exactly where he was going. He led Eric to a deep hollow, fronted by a wall of rock that would hide them from the ocean.

They reached it just in time. A moment later, a small motorboat came around the rocky point and Eric, peering through a peephole in the rocks, could see Kimo looking through his binoculars, scanning the shore. He ducked back and kept a tight hold on Popoki, who was struggling to get out of his arms.

"It's Kimo and Aleka," he told Kala, who lay on his stomach at the far end of the cave. "Shhh! Your voice goes good across water," Kala whispered.

The sound of the motor and the voices of Kimo and Aleka resounded in the cave for a long time as the boat went around the cove. Eric crouched next to the wall, holding Popoki so she wouldn't run outside and give them away, and hoping she wouldn't make any sound. At last the sound of the boat faded in the distance.

"They've gone," Eric said, relieved.

But Kala stayed where he was.

"They be back. They go search along coast, come back this way."

Eric wondered how long he'd have to hide like this. He tried to find a comfortable position and ended up sitting on the ground with the cat on his lap. She had given up struggling and gone to sleep with her head in the crook of his elbow and he left her there, glad she was staying quiet.

Kala laughed at her.

"That no wild cat. It belong to you for sure. When they put you in shed, she hung around outside. Wouldn't go away for nothing."

"Well, she really isn't mine. She came with a boat I borrowed from some friends."

"What you do when we swam here? Carry her?"

"I don't know how she followed us. I think she might have gone along the cliff beside us. Anyway, she just turned up while we were sleeping."

Kala laughed again.

"Good thing she not afraid of water. I got boat hidden near here. We get to it soon."

"Where are we going then?"

"Up coast, to place Pele don't know about."

Eric scratched Popoki's damp fur thoughtfully.

"You're going to leave Eden, too?"

"For sure. I no can go back. I stole key to shed from Pele's desk while everybody eating. She know now I got you out of there." He frowned at the rocky floor of the cave. "When those two guys go back, tell her we got away, she send out fire and storms after us. Try to kill us."

"How could she send fire and storms after us? What do you mean?"

Kala's brown eyes were very serious.

"That Pele, she powerful *kahuna*. She goddess Pele in new body. You know about Pele?"

"You mean the goddess of volcanoes? Sure I know about her, but she was only a legend."

Kala shrugged.

"You think that, okay. But I know. Pele make Diamond Head spout up fire like Mauna Loa, punish wicked people in Waikiki."

"Pele didn't do that. She's just trying to make you all believe she's got supernatural powers. She's crazy!"

It made sense, now, the chanting Pele had done when he was there, and the hypnotic spell she seemed to have over those teenagers.

Kala was shaking his head.

"You *haoles* will go way from Hawaii when she make fire and storms. Then everyone else here die if they not go way. Only Children of Eden will live, start new world here in Hawaii. Good world. Only Eden be safe from fire and destruction. Pele keep it safe. Pele has *mana*, sacred power of universe."

His words sounded almost like the chant Pele had spoken. Obviously this was a story that had been told to him many times. And this was the religion of Eden!

"If you think that, Kala, if you believe everyone in the Islands is going to be destroyed except the Children of Eden, why are you helping me? Why don't you stay in Eden, where you're supposed to be safe?"

Kala pushed a pebble with his fingers.

"I no run from Eden to help *you*. There somebody else who need me."

Eric stared at him.

"Who? Noelani?"

"For sure."

"Where is she? Is she all right?"

But now Eric could hear the motor of the returning boat, and there was no chance for Kala to answer him without giving away their hiding place.

The noise grew louder and suddenly stopped. Eric and Kala exchanged frightened glances.

The boat had stopped just outside their cave. And someone was getting out.

6 • *Pursuit*

Eric froze, too frightened to move. He gripped Popoki tightly and prayed she would stay quiet, as he and Kala waited and listened.

Outside the cave they could hear the two men talking a short distance away.

"She gonna be mad if we come back without them." It was Aleka's voice.

"They not here. You saw sharks out there. No way they get out of cove in one piece." Kimo sounded impatient.

"We gotta look. All these places to hide along here. We gotta look in them."

"So you gonna look in every one? That take all day, *pupule*. Come on. I hungry."

"Hold on, Kimo. Must look for them, for sure they're not here." Aleka's voice faded out with a slight echo, as though he'd entered one of the caves.

A moment passed while Eric held his breath, then Kimo spoke again.

"See? They no here. Sharks got 'em. I told you. Come on!"

Eric squeezed his eyes shut and nodded silent agreement with Kimo. *Go, Aleka! Go back to Eden and get your breakfast. Go!*

But Aleka's voice swelled and faded again, closer this time. "Hey, maybe this is hiding place. Big tunnel here."

Eric was so nervous that he accidently squeezed the cat. She jerked away from him and ran toward the entrance to their hiding place, then stopped, her back arched, her tail stiff.

Eric's breath caught in his throat. If the cat moved a few inches farther, she'd be visible from outside. Cautiously, he leaned forward, trying not to startle her into running away. She watched him, her eyes suspicious, as he slowly reached out his hands. Moving carefully, he gently pulled her to him, holding her inside his shirt against his chest. Now she squirmed in a frantic attempt to get away, but the struggle was brief and silent. Eric held her fast.

Finally there was the sound of the motor starting and Kimo shouting, "Come on, *pupule*! You stay here, then you gotta swim back!"

"Okay. Okay!"

Eric heard the thump of Aleka's feet in the boat, then the roar of the motor as the boat sped past them, the sound fading away.

Popoki screeched a loud, indignant protest.

Eric laughed and released her, and Kala got up grinning.

"Hey, that one good cat you got there. She keep quiet at right time."

Eric bent to pet her. "Okay, Popoki. I didn't hurt you. Good girl."

"Come on," Kala said. "We go now."

Eric glanced at the sun as they went outside, guessing it to be about seven o'clock high.

"All that talking about breakfast," he groaned. "I'm hungry. Thirsty, too."

Kala went to the edge of the rocks and plunged his hands into the water while Eric watched curiously. In a moment he had pried a small, dome-shaped shellfish from a rock and was holding it up.

"Here," he said. "Do it like this." He reached inside the shell with his thumb, scraped out the meat, and popped it into his mouth.

"Opihi," he said. "Good stuff."

Eric knelt beside him, and soon his fingers found some of the creatures clinging to the rocks. Eating raw and squirming shellfish wasn't his idea of a good substitute for bacon and eggs, but he was so hungry the seafood tasted great. After he'd eaten several, he gave some to Popoki. The cat batted the first one across the rock with her paw, then sniffed at it suspiciously. Apparently she liked the smell, for she downed it and meowed for more.

When their hunger was somewhat satisfied, they headed for the center of the cove, walking among the formations the sea had carved.

"You were going to tell me about Noelani," Eric said.

"She not far away."

"Here in this cove?"

"No. Not here."

Kala jumped off the ledge and trotted through a patch of huge ferns. He seemed reluctant to talk about Noelani, and Eric wondered why. But at least he'd find out for himself soon what was going on. The thought of seeing her again was exciting. He wanted to hear what happened to her on Oahu.

Kala led them to a clearing where a stream of water emptied into a dark, sparkling pool. They drank from it, the cat lapping daintily at its edge, then they went on through the forest to a place where mountain apples and guava grew. They picked some as they made their way back toward the beach. There, about fifty feet from the water, Kala pushed aside a pile of elephant-ear leaves and palm fronds under a tree, and Eric saw the boat.

It was a light, homemade catamaran. The two pontoons were logs lashed with rope to the raft that formed the deck. The sail was neatly folded on the deck, the mast resting beside it in three sections that could be fitted together. There were paddles and a fishing pole secured to the pontoons.

"I made it," Kala said. "Took many months."

His broad face glowed with pride.

"It looks great."

Eric walked around it, admiring.

"Nobody know about it. I work on it in secret. Some days I swim out here to do it, like we just did."

"In spite of the sharks? I heard Kimo say he saw some in the bay."

Kala shrugged.

"They not come near me. Well—maybe little ones." He laughed. "Hey, I keep close to cliff when I swim here. Then I get out of water fast if I have to."

Eric ran his fingers over one of the smoothly-planed paddles. "Yeah, this boat is all right! Why don't you want Pele to know about it?"

Kala's eyes became wary. "Maybe I tell you later. Right now I only know you friend to Noelani."

"Sure, that's okay. I wasn't trying to be nosy. But I'm your friend, too." Eric held out his hand. "You saved my life, Kala. I'll always be your friend."

84

Kala turned away, ignoring the outstretched hand.

"I make gods angry when I save your life. Pele say you sacrifice for gods. *Kapu wela* sacred ceremony. I cheat gods out of their sacrifice." He turned toward Eric again, his brown eyes narrowed. "I not cheat gods for you."

"For Noelani?"

"For Noelani. Maybe for me, too." He went to one of the log pontoons and began dragging it. "You pull that one. Must get this in water."

They half-pulled, half-carried the boat through the underbrush to the shore. Eric wondered what Kala meant. If Kala had saved him only because he was Noelani's friend, then Kala must feel Noelani needed him now—that Eric could do something for her Kala couldn't do himself. But what? Why did she need Eric's help?

At the edge of the sea, Kala fitted the mast together, and Eric helped him rig the sail. Then, together, they waded into the rocky surf.

Eric had been so busy with the boat and his own thoughts that he had forgotten about the cat. When the shelf under their feet dropped off and they were clambering onto the catamaran, Eric saw her. She was standing halfway in the water, her fur soaked by the waves that lapped at her, watching them with sad yellow eyes.

He dived into the water and went back for her.

"Here," he said, settling her around his neck. "Hold on."

It was low tide and the surf was light, but he could feel her, frightened, dig her claws into his shoulder as he boarded the boat. When he set her down, she shook herself then began to lick herself dry.

Kala swung the sail to catch the breeze, and the boat

skimmed easily to the mouth of the cove, turning eastward to follow the line of the shore. For a while, Eric had to squint, since the sun was bright ahead of them, but soon dark clouds were covering it and a light rain began.

"Wind rising," Kala muttered, struggling with the tiller.

A strong gust hit them, and the little boat veered and tipped, then righted itself. Eric, sitting cross-legged, held onto the side of the raft. The cat flattened herself on the deck, clawing the wood.

Eric looked out across the water and saw something that made his heart jump. A few yards away, a fin jutted out of the murky waves.

"Shark!" he cried out.

Kala jerked his head around to see, and together they watched the long oval body speeding straight for them as the boat, tiller swinging, tipped again. Eric, off balance, pitched forward and fell into the water. He went under and came up, spluttering. The boat was speeding away from him, and his heart jumped again as he saw the fin heading toward him. He remembered to stay calm, to try to look like a floating dead thing, not a live meal. He looked to see where the shark was. It had disappeared. Kala was laughing.

"Ulua," he said.

"Why are you laughing? You think it's funny I almost got eaten by a shark?"

"That no shark. That *ulua.* I try to tell you."

"What's *ulua*?"

"Fish with big hump head. Narrow, not wide like shark. It no eat you. *You* eat *it*."

"Oh," Eric said. "Very funny."

The rain was falling harder now, and the wind rising.

86

A huge clap of thunder sounded and Eric turned his head to see lightning bolts arching and leaping to the west, lighting the dark sky with fierce intensity. The little boat rocked as it raced ahead.

He could barely hear what Kala muttered repeatedly.

"Pele is angry."

So Kala thought Pele was sending fire and storms after them. Eric tried to understand what was in Kala's mind. Maybe if he'd been brainwashed like Kala had, he'd feel the same way about the many strange things that were happening.

But then, the volcano on Oahu could have something to do with the storms and earthquakes, Eric decided. The earth was heaving, spewing out fire into the atmosphere, disrupting everything in the area. The catamaran was sliding into the troughs between the swelling waves, then tossing up to their crests, only to slip down again. How long could this craft take this rough treatment?

Eric raised his voice against the wind. "How much farther?"

Kala was too busy to answer, hanging onto the tiller with both hands, steering inward toward another cove, guarded by rocky pillars. Somehow the catamaran sailed past them safely, skidded toward the pebbly shore and then, as Eric and Kala struggled to furl the sail, it tipped into the water, the mast scraping along the rocky shallows.

Eric landed in the water, Kala beside him. Popoki went past them in a white flash, leaping for the shore, her four legs spread wildly. Pounded by the waves, Kala and Eric managed to struggle to their feet, catch the boat, and tow it to land.

"It's not damaged much," Eric said after he'd examined the mast and sails.

The tip of the mast had cracked, and the sails were soaked, but everything else seemed sound. They pulled the boat high enough so that the waves could not do further damage.

Popoki, her tail switching, huddled under a clump of fern, closing her eyes against the pelting rain.

"Is this where we find Noelani?" Eric asked Kala.

"She not far." Kala pointed to a stream that emptied into a pool among the rocks. "We follow that."

Ohia trees and pandanus formed a canopy over their heads as they followed a goat trail up the gentle slope. Another clap of thunder, and the cat jumped from her shelter to go with them, this time staying close to their legs. The tropical rain, which seemed to be dying down now, pattered through the leaves. Here and there, fragrant white ginger blossoms hung over the places where the stream pooled, and Eric, catching the fragrance, thought of Noelani. She wouldn't expect to see him here. What would she say? Did she want to see him as much as he wanted to see her? Impatiently, he tried to hurry on the slippery trail, digging his bare toes into the mud.

He figured they had traveled about a mile before they came to the old shack. It stood on the edge of a small cliff, mauna loa vines growing over its rock walls and palm-thatched roof, and around its sagging door. They stopped in front of the steps leading to the door, rain drizzling down on them, and Kala turned to Eric.

"Noelani in here." His face was grave.

Eric nodded and started toward the door, but Kala caught his arm to stop him. "She different now. Not like she was before."

His expression and his voice made Eric feel very strange indeed.

"Different? What do you mean, Kala?"

The words seemed hard for Kala to say, but he finally got them out.

"You like Noelani, right?"

Eric nodded.

"Then don't make her sad. Okay?"

Kala turned quickly and went up the steps to knock at the ancient door.

He had to knock twice, banging hard on the rotten wood before it was opened a crack, and Eric heard Noelani's voice. "Go away, Kala."

"Hey, come on. It wet out here. We come long way," Kala pleaded.

Standing behind him, Eric tried to see through the crack as it opened half an inch wider, but the inside of the hut was dark, and he couldn't make out Noelani's face. But he heard her gasp of surprise.

"Eric! Why did you bring him here, Kala?"

What was the matter with her, Eric wondered. She'd been happy to see him when they met in the marketplace.

"Noelani, please let us in," he called.

Kala pushed at the door, trying to open it wider.

"Noelani, don't be *pupule*. Let us in."

But she held the door against him. "I don't want to see anybody. Go away." She sounded angry now.

Eric tried again. "I've been to Eden, Noelani. I'd like to tell you about it. Can't we come in out of the rain and talk?"

"You went to Eden?" She sounded surprised.

"Sure," Eric said. "No way we can go back there, either. Want to hear about it?"

There was a silence before the girl spoke again.

"Okay. Give me a minute. Then you can come in. But just for a little while."

She closed the door again and Eric and Kala waited.

"What is it? What's the matter with her?" Eric asked quietly.

"Wait. You see," was all he would say.

In a few moments they heard Noelani calling. "Okay. You can come in."

The room was small and dim. Eric could see a rough table with benches in the center of the room, bunks on either side, and beyond that a doorway to a room that appeared to be a kitchen. He looked around for Noelani. The scent of wild ginger was the only sign of her presence.

"Noelani?"

"I'm in here. You stay there." Her voice came from the kitchen.

"Why won't you let me see you?"

"If you're hungry, I've made some *lau-lau,*" she said ignoring his question. "It's on the table. I'll stay in here. Eric, tell me what happened when you went to Eden."

"This is dumb—you staying in there where we can't see you, and us out here."

"Please! Just stay there!" She sounded close to tears.

He looked at Kala, hoping he could coax her to come out, but the Hawaiian was sitting down at the table, lifting the lid of a large iron pot. "Here," he handed Eric a little bundle wrapped in a leaf, then took one for himself.

Puzzled, but hungry, Eric sat down and bit into the food. It was warm and delicious, about the size of a hot dog, the leaf wrapped around cooked meat and something that tasted like spinach.

While they ate, he told Noelani about his fall from the helicopter and his adventures since then, ending with his experience with Pele in Eden. Kala interrupted every now and then to supply his own version of what had happened. Eric could hear a gasp from Noelani when he came to the part where Pele decided to sacrifice him in the fire.

"Oh, Eric! Then the gods are angry with you, too!"

"The gods aren't angry with me. That crazy woman, Pele, is. She has some wild idea that you and I are plotting against her and her colony. She said I was planning to bring friends to break up her little group."

His last words were lost in a rumble of thunder. A lightning flash lit the kitchen, so that Eric could see the girl's silhouette. Almost as soon as the flash died, the building began to shake. The iron pot thumped on the table. The bunks rattled and creaked and the floor danced under Eric's feet.

Noelani screamed in fright and ran out of the kitchen toward him. She flung herself against him and hid her face on his shoulder; he put his arms around her. She was shivering.

"It's okay. Look, the quake's stopping now. It's all right."

"She's after us! She's going to kill us!" Her voice was a muffled sob.

"You mean Pele? No way!"

He glanced at Kala. The Hawaiian had his head buried in his arms, as though waiting for a final blow.

"Hey," Eric said. "It's okay. Just a little quake."

Kala cautiously looked up, around the room, then back at Eric. "Pele!" He made the word sound frightening.

"Just aftershocks," Eric said. He wished they'd both stop being so sure it was Pele doing all these things. He was almost believing it himself. "Probably from that quake and the volcano on Oahu. It's all over now."

Noelani suddenly pulled out of his arms, clapped her hands over her face and whirled around, stumbling toward the kitchen.

"Hey! Wait a minute!"

He caught her arm to stop her.

She struggled to get free. "Let me go!"

"What are you running away for? Tell me what's the matter."

"I don't want you to see me like this."

She kept her hands over her face.

"Whatever it is, it won't matter to me. We're friends, aren't we? Nothing's going to change that."

But even as Eric tried to reassure her, a pit of apprehension widened in his stomach. Something awful had happened to her. And he had to know what it was.

Suddenly there was a crashing sound in the kitchen, and the tinkle of broken glass. They looked up, startled to see Popoki running toward them. She must have found a place to get in, Eric thought, and knocked over a glass as she did so. He turned his attention to Noelani. She was staring at the cat, startled, and her hands had dropped from her face. Eric felt horror at what he saw.

On one side of her face, crawling across her cheek from the eye to the chin, was the red, ugly outline of a snake.

7 • *Noelani*

Eric couldn't help staring at Noelani's face. Tears welled up in her eyes as she looked at him, but she stood there, making no further attempt to hide the terrible snake-picture on her cheek. Bloated and discolored, it seemed to be burned into her skin.

"Who did that to you?" Eric demanded.

"Pele. It was punishment."

Pele! He might have known it would be that monster.

"But why? Why did she want to punish you?"

"Because she knew about our meeting in the marketplace. Because I talked to you there, and gave you the special lei."

She seemed to be trying to hold back tears, and her voice quivered.

Eric wanted to cry, too. He wanted to scream threats against Pele and her cruelty. But he spoke gently to Noelani, to try to calm her. "Sit down." He motioned her to the bench, across from Kala, and sat beside her. "Would you tell me about it?"

She shrugged, brushing away her tears.

"Where do you want me to start?"

"Tell me what you did after the quake on Oahu. I searched the whole marketplace for you and couldn't find you anywhere."

She sighed.

"That seems like such a long time ago. I was so surprised to see you, and so happy. But one of those men was watching me—"

"What men?"

"Those men who watch us girls when we go to other islands to sell our leis. Pele's friends live in those places. They watch to make sure we're all right. We don't know when they're watching us, but Pele says they're always there if we need them."

Eric felt doubtful. "But you seemed to be afraid of that man. If he was just there to help you, why were you afraid of him?"

She lifted her dark eyebrows. "Because he would tell Pele about the lei I gave you. That was wrong. I wasn't supposed to do that. But I wanted you to have the best flowers to welcome you to Hawaii."

Eric tried to remember.

"It was a lei of orchids, wasn't it?"

"Yes, I gave you the special lei. Eden orchids. They grow only in Eden, that's why they're the most expensive. We usually get fifty dollars for those."

Eric whistled.

"What a rip-off!"

"Well, they're very special flowers, and the leis are made carefully—different from the others. We have regular customers for them. Some people buy two and three of them at a time, but most people just buy the other leis, the ones that cost less."

94

"So the man watching you in the marketplace reported to Pele that you gave me one?"

"Yes. That's why she was so angry."

"That's funny," Eric said. "That's really weird. Why would she get so mad about a bunch of flowers, even if they were the expensive ones? And if that man was only supposed to be there to help you, what's he doing telling tales to Pele about you?"

"I don't understand either," Noelani said. "There are a lot of strange things about Pele I don't understand." She and Kala exchanged a look that Eric couldn't interpret, but when neither of them said anything more, he didn't press the subject. It wouldn't do any good. "So where did you go when the quake happened, after we met in the marketplace?"

"The man told me to go right back to our boat and get off the island. I was afraid to wait for you. I knew Pele was already starting to destroy Honolulu and the rest of Oahu, and we had to go right back to Eden."

"But Pele wasn't causing the volcano!" And while Noelani and Kala listened with disbelief, Eric tried to explain. "See, my dad told me about the big land masses that cover the whole earth. When they collide—" It was obvious they didn't want to listen and wouldn't be convinced, so he gave up. "Never mind. Just go on, Noelani. You went back to the boat and returned to Eden?"

She twisted a strand of her long hair nervously.

"Yes. That man radioed to her right away, and when I got back, Pele already knew I'd seen you. She was furious. She accused me of telling you lies about Eden. She said all sorts of things, just like she said to you. She called me the serpent in Eden." Her scarred face grew somber as she spoke.

"That's when she did this." Her fingers touched her cheek and her voice trembled.

It was a moment before she could go on. "She got Kimo and Aleka to take me to the place of the fire, and she talked about throwing me into it. Then she decided not to. I think she was afraid you might be looking for me, Eric. If she sacrificed me in the fire you might find out about it. So she got a big metal bracelet out of her jewelry box—one made like a snake—and she put wire on it and tied it to a poker—and heated it in the fire, and—"

Her voice broke and she put her head into her hands and sobbed, unable to go on.

Kala took up her story, his voice strangely cold.

"Kimo and Aleka hold her down while Pele burn that thing into her face. I hear her scream, all the way to where we fish off rocks on beach. Everybody hear. We all run to Pele's house to see what go on. Pele say snake just show up on Noelani's face. She say it mean Noelani evil."

Eric felt a wave of nausea mix with his anger.

"Don't tell me they believed her!"

Kala shook his head.

"Not me. Maybe others think that. I don't know."

"If I ever meet Pele again," Eric said furiously, "I'll see she gets what's coming to her."

Noelani shook her head emphatically.

"No. Don't talk like that, Eric. She can destroy everyone with her *mana*. No one can hurt her."

Eric knew there was no use arguing with her—not here—not now. Some other time, when they were safe and Noelani knew she didn't have to be afraid anymore—maybe then he could convince them both that Pele was only human.

"Well she's not going to hurt any of us any more," he said firmly. "And how did you get here?"

"Kala brought me. Pele told Kimo to take me out in the boat and shove me into the ocean. She said if I didn't die there, she would chase me with fire and wind, that the gods were against me now. I can never again be one of the chosen."

As if to prove what she said, there was a terrific thunderclap, and the little hut shook again for a moment, while the rain pelted against the roof. In the silence that followed, Eric heard the cry of a cat, and looked down to see Popoki huddled by his feet.

"Where did it come from?" Noelani asked, and listened intently as Eric explained about Popoki. Eric was grateful for a change of subject.

Noelani found a piece of torn blanket on one of the bunks and dried the cat with it, forgetting herself for the first time since they'd been here. Kala broke off a piece of *lau-lau* to offer the animal. Then Noelani sat on the edge of one of the bunks with the cat purring in her lap.

Eric was impatient to hear the rest of her story.

"Tell me how you got to this cabin. How did Kala save you?"

"I told Kimo I would give him my opal ring if he would take me to Kalaupapa. It's a very precious ring that belonged to my mother. Kimo liked it. He took the ring, but he just let me off on the rocks by the cove."

"Then how did you get here?"

"I find her," Kala said. "When Kimo take her away, I swim to where my boat is. I wait till he come back alone. Then I take my boat to go look for Noelani."

"He found me down among the rocks," Noelani said. "I think I was nearly dead then. He brought me here, to this old shack he knew about."

"People live here long time ago," Kala said. "They all gone now. Old ones die and young ones move to where they have lights and music and stores. Other houses here gone now too. But this old one made of stone. It last. I been here sometimes to hunt wild pig."

"Does Pele know about it?" Eric asked him.

"Maybe. I don't know."

Eric wondered if he, too, was beginning to believe in Pele's powerful *mana*. He found himself worrying that she might find them here. But that was dumb. How could she? She probably thought they were all lost in the ocean.

"So you brought her here, Kala, and then went back to Eden?"

"For sure. Pele not know I find Noelani. She not even know I went away from Eden. I go back only to find out things."

"What things?"

Kala's thick, black eyebrows met over his nose in a frown. "Whatever. Why Pele so worried that she does that to Noelani. And other things I wonder about, too."

"Tell him Kala," Noelani urged, but he shook his head.

"You tell," he said. "I go pick fruit. Still hungry."

"You're going out in this storm?" Eric asked, but Kala was gone. Eric grinned at Noelani. "Oh well, we've been wet ever since we left Eden. I guess he doesn't mind a little more water. But I get the feeling Kala doesn't like me much, even though he saved my life, too."

"You're a *haole*. Pele taught us never to trust *haoles!*"

"But you seem to trust me, Noelani."

She smiled for the first time, the scar twisting her lovely cheek.

98

"When I first saw you at the White House that day, I liked you, so I wrote to you. Then I saw your face in a magazine in a tourist shop. You were part of another world—so different from Eden. You're handsome and famous, and you do exciting things. I wanted to hear all about that world of yours outside of Eden," she said wistfully.

"Pele said that Hawaii was going to be separated from all the rest of the world. Everything else was going to be destroyed. That meant I would never have a chance to see other parts of it. That made me sad."

She looked down at the cat and stroked it gently. "That's when I began to write to you. When you sent letters back, I felt close to you. I—I liked your telling me about where you went and what you did. And I liked you a lot." She looked down, embarrassed by her own frankness.

Eric saw her scarred face and felt pain for what she must be feeling. There was an awkward silence.

She smiled sadly, then spoke again. "I will stay here, in this cabin now. I will never see anyone. I don't need anyone."

"You can't do that . . . hide away here like a hermit."

"Why not?"

"Because you're young, and—" Eric broke off, embarrassed.

"Beautiful?" She laughed, and her laughter was almost a cry.

"Of course you're beautiful," Eric told her. "You were tortured and scarred, but there's plastic surgery that can fix your face so it's just like it used to be."

She shook her head.

"I won't go to any doctor. I've got some herbs that are helping my skin. We didn't have any doctors in Eden, so we learned to let nature heal us. Anyway, I'd have to explain to a doctor what happened, and I can't do that.''

"Why not?''

"If Pele found out—''

Eric got up and paced the room, angrily. "You've got to stop being so afraid of her, Noelani, and you've got to go away with us. As soon as I can get to the ranch and find my dad, we can get you to a doctor.''

As he walked across the floor, he heard a long low rumble. Thunder? No, this was a roar that came from the center of the earth. The floor began to rock, and the walls seemed to be leaning inward. They were going to tumble down on top of them! In one swift, panicked movement he reached for Noelani, yanked her to her feet, and shoved her under the table, then crawled under it beside her.

Now the hut was indeed falling around them. Pieces of walls and ceiling thudded against the tabletop and crashed to the floor. The ground was turning and twisting under them. The table was rocking. Noelani gave a frightened cry, and pressed herself against him while Eric closed his eyes and prayed that the old table-top would not collapse on them.

A sound like a giant explosion made him turn his head to see the iron pot that had held the lau-laus on the table—crash through the flooring. A screech from the cat behind him turned into a wail of terror, mingled with the clang of collapsing metal.

The whole cabin must be crumbling, judging by the noise. He held one arm around Noelani in an attempt to shield her, and waited, shivering, for whatever might come.

Then it was over.

The ground stopped shaking. Something thudded and

100

rolled across the floor. He heard the tinkle of broken glass in the kitchen. Then silence. He opened his eyes to see white dust whirling around them. Coughing, he crawled out from the shelter and surveyed the damage.

Through the haze he could see one of the walls had disintegrated into a heap of rubble. The bunks had disappeared under wood and stone. Sections of the floor were gone where falling stone and metal had broken through it. Looking up, he could see that the roof had been torn raggedly, leaving a gap that let in the rain.

Noelani came out from under the table and stood beside him, grasping his arm with frightened fingers.

"Pele! She's come after us!"

"Not Pele, it's another earthquake. Another aftershock."

Eric's words echoed oddly through the ruins. He reached down to rub a spot on his leg where the cat had clawed him under the table in her fright.

Then he remembered Kala. "We'd better look for Kala," he said. "Then we'll get away from here."

Noelani spoke quietly, but her voice was tight with terror.

"Where can we go? She'll find us anywhere."

"We're alive, aren't we?" Eric spoke impatiently. "She didn't kill us. That quake didn't even hurt us. Look—it didn't even hurt the cat." He looked down into the girl's shadowed eyes. "If Pele's trying to kill us, she's goofed it up pretty badly."

Noelani didn't answer, but she held his arm as they made their way to the front door. It dangled on its top hinge. Eric pushed it back, allowing them to step through the doorway.

The rain had subsided to a fine drizzle now, and a rainbow arched in the western sky over the emerald trees.

The scene was calm and reassuring, as though nothing but beauty could exist here; as though the terrors of the past days could never have happened. Eric took a deep breath of fresh air to clear his lungs. The three front steps of the cabin were standing solidly. They stood on the top one, calling Kala's name, but there was no response.

He looked around, to see where the Hawaiian might have gone. The earthquake didn't seem to have done much damage out here. Only a few dead branches were shaken loose from the trees. Popoki streaked past him in a flash of white, and scurried down the trail beside the stream, chasing something he couldn't see. In the distance, he heard the plaintive call of wild goats.

"Where do you think Kala might have gone?" he asked Noelani.

"There are guava trees over that way. He might be there."

They walked among the trees, calling every now and then, hearing no answer. Eric was getting worried. They went farther into the rain forest and searched for a long time without success. Finally they stopped to rest and eat some wild cherries they'd picked along the way.

"We've got to find him." Eric squinted up at the sun that was hanging low over the western cliff. "It'll be dark soon."

Tilting her head to listen, Noelani raised her hand for silence. "What's that?"

Eric strained to hear. It was a voice—surely Kala's— shouting, a long way off. They both got up and ran toward the sound. They were close to the cliff, now, that rose sheer above them. Where was he? Eric called again, and the answer came faint and hoarse. They clambered over a ridge of rocks, and past the waterfall leaping over them, until they were standing at the edge of a deep ravine.

Eric looked down. The ravine was a fresh deep slash at the foot of the cliff, bordered by rocks, a grassy field beyond it. About twenty feet below him, Eric could see Kala lying beside a big rock. He was on a small sloping jut of land. Below the jut, the ravine plunged steeply. Eric felt dizzy as he looked. Kala's feet were at the edge of the precipice, and he seemed to be clinging to the rock to keep from falling.

Noelani put words to Eric's fears.

"He can't climb out of there. He'll go over that cliff if he tries."

"Maybe we can throw a vine or something down there to help him up." Eric looked around to find one, but there were no trees here and no vines; only the rocks and the grass.

"Hold on," he shouted down to Kala. "We'll get you out of there."

Kala's answer was hoarse and pained. "My arm. I can't get loose."

Now Eric realized that the big rock lying by Kala's shoulder was pinning his arm to the ground. There was no way he could climb out of there by himself.

Eric saw no way he could get down there to help him. Even if he did somehow make it, both of them might slide off the ledge. Or it could crumble under them. But Eric knew he had to do something. Fast.

"Lord, I've got another problem, and I don't see any way to solve it. But I can't just leave Kala down there—"

8 • *Descent Toward Death*

Noelani was moaning, rocking back and forth with her grief. Eric realized her religion gave her no hope, only fear. As he watched her there, a great sadness filled his heart.

But there was no time to comfort her now. He called words of assurance to Kala as he knelt at the edge of the ravine. Eric realized he was praying, not only with quiet words, but with his whole being. The sun was behind the cliff now, dropping long shadows that would soon join to become darkness.

While Eric was testing the edge of the embankment with his hands, Popoki appeared. She had managed to follow them again, and came running up to him with a delighted meow. He picked her up and absentmindedly tucked her warm furry body inside his shirt as he contemplated what to do next.

When he put his hand inside his shirt, his fingers touched the rope he had taken with him from the *Kamalo,* still coiled around his waist. He had become so accustomed to its being there he had forgotten about it!

Quickly he pulled his shirt up and began to unwind the nylon rope. Noelani, surprised but eager, helped him unfasten the knot that held it.

"We're going to get you out!" she called down to Kala.

Eric experienced a stab of doubt when he realized the rope was probably only fifteen, maybe eighteen feet long. It was sturdy, braided nylon and would hold a man's weight, but would it be long enough to reach Kala some twenty feet below? There was only one way to find out. He searched for something to anchor the end of the rope.

There were no trees, but he found a big, solidly-set boulder about four feet back from the edge of the ravine, and Noelani helped him loop and fasten the rope around it. Together they pulled with all their strength to test it. The boulder and the knot seemed secure. To save rope, Eric decided against a harness, so he looped the other end of it through his belt and tied it there. Then he looked over the edge.

The ravine seemed to be a straight wall of earth and rock; a bottomless pit dropping sheerly into blackness. Looking down made his head whirl and he turned away, trying to steady himself. He wouldn't be able to look down once he went over that edge. If he let himself get dizzy, let himself think about what lay under him, he might never make it. But of course there was a rope holding him. And Kala lying helpless, waiting for him. He'd have to go now.

His mind began a conversation of prayer with the God who promises to be an "ever present help" to His children. Eric knelt at the edge and dropped one bare foot behind him, searching for a toehold. Noelani

watched him anxiously as he felt a firm patch of rock under his foot and put his weight on it. It held, and he grasped the yielding cliffside with both hands while his other foot sought someplace to rest. One hand slipped and he grabbed out with it, his fingers finding a niche to hold, to steady his body close to the cliff face. But his foot could find nothing—nowhere to step. Warily, he stretched his leg lower, trying not to look down. Still there was no place to set his foot. He would have to look, to find niches and footholds and rocky outcroppings, otherwise the climb down would take too long. The light was fading. He had to get to Kala as quickly as possible.

Keeping his body close to the cliff, he looked down, searching the places just below his feet, careful not to look all the way into that dizzying distance. There—he could see an indentation to the right of his free foot. Carefully he stepped into it, tested it, and found it solid. He clutched the rope, first with one hand, then with the other. Now he could crawl down its length, placing his feet wherever he could find a hold for them, but keeping his weight on the rope. Bits of loose earth and rock shook loose as he traveled, and he shouted to Kala to cover his face with his free arm.

Finally he was at the end of the rope, feeling the tug at his waist, his feet planted firmly against the side of the ravine, his hands grasping the nylon.

He turned his head slowly to look down.

Kala lay about ten feet directly below him. He could see the dark eyes watching him, and the grimace of pain on his face. The ledge where he lay was barely large enough to hold him and the boulder that pinned his arm. Eric knew he would be adding his weight to the already overburdened shelf.

"Don't think about that," Eric told himself. *"Untie*

the knot of rope. Hold it now and move your feet carefully along the face of the cliff so you'll drop beside Kala, not on top of him. Okay—now go!''

The earth shook with the impact of his weight as he landed just behind Kala's head. He looked up to see Noelani, smiling and waving her hands in a gesture of triumph. He turned his attention to Kala.

The Hawaiian lay watching him silently. Eric moved quickly to the rock that pinned him there by the lower part of his right arm and hand. Eric pushed it with both hands, but it did not budge. He would have to move closer to where it lay, right on the brink of the little shelf. If he rolled it, it would drop into the abyss. He edged carefully toward it until he could get his whole body against it, then he pushed again, muscles straining.

The rock didn't budge.

"Try again," Kala said. "I help." He swung his feet into position to push at the rock with them, bending his knees, moaning with the effort and the tearing pain of his arm and hand.

Eric tensed, readying himself to shove the rock along with Kala. Suddenly he heard a soft, tearing sound and the ground dropped under him. In one sickening flash he knew the ledge was breaking off and that he would fall with it. His body already tensed, he threw himself sideways, clawing for something to hold. His fingers plowed into the soft earth; his body was safely stretched out on it, but underneath his legs the support was gone and his feet dangled in space. He wasn't sure who it was that screamed. He only knew he was still on solid ground, lying behind Kala's head. For a moment he stayed there, gasping for breath. Finally he turned to see what had happened. The boulder was gone. Kala lay with his right arm hanging over the chasm. A whole chunk

108

of the ledge had been torn away along with the rock. Eric grabbed Kala's good arm, pulling Kala away from the crumbling edge of the shelf.

Now the Hawaiian was moving under his own power, hunching himself against the cliff face beside Eric, while another piece of their perch peeled away from the edge and dropped. Shivering with fear, they sat there, gasping and panting, hoping the last three feet of earth where they huddled would stay fastened to the cliff.

Finally, all movement stopped except the pounding of Eric's heart. They were safe, but for how long? The extra weight that had torn away the outer part of the ledge might break the rest of it loose at any moment. And if there should be another quake before they could get to safety—a person could go crazy thinking like this. They had to climb away from here. Now!

Eric stood up slowly, grasping at the side of the cliff. Kala, too, got carefully to his feet. His right arm was covered with blood. His face shone with sweat. His eyes were black with fear. But he grinned, his teeth gleaming white in the twilight. "Thanks," he said.

"Sure." Eric grinned back, then pointed to the rope that swung above them. "Get up on my shoulders and fasten that around you. And make it quick, will you?"

He braced his back against the side of the cliff and crouched.

Kala managed to get up on his shoulders with no trouble, but it seemed like an eternity, while Eric waited and prayed, before Kala said, "Okay. I tied up now." Slowly the pressure went off Eric's shoulders. He looked up and saw the bare feet above him gripping rocky outcroppings, while Kala's good hand grasped a scraggy bush. It looked as though he'd be able to climb, even with one arm hanging by his side.

Eric swiftly found handholds and footholds for himself, right behind Kala, glad to get off that precarious perch. Now all they had to do was get up those twenty feet of cliff. But he wouldn't think about that just yet. One step at a time. Just the way he'd come down. But there'd been a rope around him then. Now there was nothing to hold him if he fell. He'd drop right into that bottomless hole.

"No—don't think that way. Lord, help me find the way up this thing. Here's a handhold between two rocks." Eric continued his running commentary with himself and the Lord.

He pressed his body against the cliff face and moved one of his feet carefully upward to find a foothold. There—a solid place. He put his weight on that foot and swung the other foot free, searching for a niche, a rock, anything to bear its weight. Just then a stone Kala must have loosened hit against his forehead. It was only a glancing blow, but it stunned him for a moment. One hand slipped away from the rock he was holding. Clawing at the wall of earth, Eric groped to find a protruding rock that would give him a handhold. He reached toward the solid knob where Kala's foot had been, and gripped it to steady himself. He breathed out the air his tight lungs had been holding and stayed there, waiting for Kala to move higher.

"God, I still need Your help." He prayed quietly. "How glad I am that You're here to give Kala and me strength to make it to the top. We sure can't do it without You! Thank You."

He wanted to call to Noelani, to tell her to wind the slackness of rope around the boulder that held it, but he decided to save the energy shouting would take. He needed every bit of strength to get up the cliff that rose above him. He hoped she would think of winding up the slack herself.

Eric was glad now that he'd kept his body in condition by lifting weights, playing tennis and handball regularly. His muscles were working smoothly and he wasn't tiring yet. But there was a stinging pain in his forehead, a throbbing pain, and now he could feel something trickling across his eyebrow and over his eyelid. That rock must have been sharp enough to cut his head as it hit him. Blood was getting in his eye, blinding him. He tried to blink it away, but was only partly successful. The bleeding became a steady trickle.

Eric couldn't let Kala get beyond his reach, even with the danger of more loosened rocks and earth dropping on him. If he should lose his hold on the cliff face, he would have to make a grab for Kala's legs and hope that the rope would hold them both. Climbing this way, close behind Kala, he could use the same rocks and niches Kala found.

The trickle of blood into his eye was annoying. The climb seemed to go on forever. Eric began to feel this was all unreal; like some nightmare of struggling endlessly upward, half-blinded by blood from his head wound, hearing the sound of his own heavy breathing echoing back to him from the face of the cliff. His tense muscles began to ache, now, but a monstrous fear drove him— the knowledge of the dark abyss underneath them and the possibility of an earthquake that would surely shake them off the face of this cliff to their death below. He sensed a creeping fear slowly enveloping him. He could not push these thoughts away. He began to hum softly —"What a Friend we have in Jesus," thinking about the words of the old hymn while he waited for Kala to make the next move.

Kala's foot moved off a rocky outcropping and he rose just above Eric's head. Eric placed his left hand on that rock and saw a niche just above it for his right hand. He thrust his fingers into it and lifted his foot to find a stepping place.

Something moved along his right hand. Startled, Eric twitched the hand involuntarily for a fraction of a second, without letting his hand leave the niche. Then he looked to see what was on his fingers.

A large spider, about the size of a quarter, moved slowly over his knuckles, its reddish-brown body covered with stiff black hairs. Revulsion made him want to jerk his hand out of the hole and shake the ugly thing off, but he couldn't. He still had only one foothold. Was it a poisonous spider? Would it sting him? He searched frantically for a place to step as he watched the spider crawl across the back of his hand and start down his arm. He clenched his teeth and ran his foot carefully up the cliff wall. Once he got a foothold he could shake it off.

At last he found one, and holding the cliff face with one hand, and with both of his feet supported, he shook his arm to knock the spider off. The movement nearly sent him off balance.

"Eric!" Noelani's voice seemed to be right next to his ear.

Startled, he looked up and saw that he was alone on the cliffside. Kala must have reached the top while he was struggling with the spider. There were only three or four feet left to go, and he would be safe at the top, too. And now the end of the rope was dangling right in front of him.

"Here," Noelani said. "Grab this. Kala and I can pull you the rest of the way."

Joyfully, Eric grasped the rope, first with one hand,

112

then with the other. He felt the pull as the rope moved him upward and he gripped the earth with his feet to help. Now his head was over the ledge, and he saw Kala tugging with his one good hand while Noelani, behind him, strained at the rope. Eric had his shoulders up to the top of the ledge. In a moment he could let go the rope and haul himself over the edge of the cliff to solid ground. Relief made him feel light and airy, so light he felt he could fly over the last little distance that remained between him and safety.

Then he heard the low rumble and felt the quivering that meant another earthquake.

9 • The Plant Puzzle

Eric felt the edge of the cliff shaking, and his joy turned to sudden fear. He was only inches from safety. Could he make it? The lower half of his body dangled over the ravine. Only his arms and shoulders were flat on the ground at the edge of the cliff. He hung onto the rope with all his strength while Noelani and Kala struggled to pull him all the way over the rim. But they were having trouble keeping on their feet as the ground shook under them, and Eric could feel the brink of the cliff loosening where his chest lay against it. Terrified, he realized that he wasn't going forward any longer; that the others were losing control of the line that could save his life.

He tried to think. If he let go of the rope and tried to use his hands to haul himself over, he might not be able to make it. If he held the rope, there were two people trying to save him. But even as he thought this, he felt himself inching backward. He had to take a chance.

He pressed his feet into the soft earth of the cliff wall and prayed they would hold there while he gripped the slackening rope with sweating hands and gave as much of a jump as he could. The rim of the cliff banged against his waist. The moment he felt that, he let go of the rope and clawed at the ground, swinging his legs up and around at the same time, trying to get them over the edge. His body twisted, but he couldn't feel solid earth under his knees. They were slipping back into emptiness, and his fingers were bringing up clods of grass, sliding back across the slick turf. He was gradually dropping backwards again over the edge of the precipice.

Through his one clear eye he could see the fear on the faces of Noelani and Kala as they dropped the useless rope and raced toward him. But they had several feet of ground to cover, and the weight of the bottom half of his body was pulling him faster over the shaking ground.

Then one of his hands, scrabbling desperately at the earth, found something solid—a protruding rock imbedded in the grass. He clung to it, stopping his backward slide.

Kala's left hand shot out, trying to catch Eric's right as it pulled away from his grasping fingers, just out of reach. Now Noelani was bending to catch Eric's other hand. She had it! He closed his fingers around her wrist with every bit of strength he had left. She wavered and almost fell, then leaned back and pulled him toward her with both hands on his left wrist, struggling against the weight of his body and the heaving ground.

So close was he to the cliff edge that Eric knew he might take her over with him if she lost her balance. He could not do that. He let go her wrist, but she tightened her hands with a visible, mighty effort, groaning and straining.

Now Kala was on his knees. He leaned forward to get Eric's other arm and grasped it. Eric came sliding over the edge of the cliff, his stomach and knees bumping over the lumpy ground and bushes with the most wonderful thumps he had ever felt in his life. Noelani and Kala wouldn't let go of Eric's arms until they had dragged him to the boulder where the rope was fastened. Then they released his hands and collapsed beside him, laughing and shouting. Eric joined in, his "Thank You. Thank You. Thank You, Lord" mixed with their howls of relief and celebration.

As Eric lay he realized the earthquake had stopped. It must have been brief and relatively gentle, Eric knew, although it had seemed to go on forever. But then, his struggle at the edge of the cliff must have taken only a minute or so, and that had seemed endless, too.

He wiped his clouded eye with the tail of his shirt and felt the cut on his forehead. It wasn't very big, and the blood was already drying. He grinned up at Popoki, who sat on top of the rock, watching them with glowing eyes.

Eric sat up. "I was afraid a couple of times that we wouldn't make it," he said. "I still can't believe we did."

"It was awful, standing up here watching," Noelani said.

"Not half as bad as climbing that cliff."

"For sure." Kala sat up, gingerly holding his right arm.

"How does it feel now?" Noelani asked him. "Is it broken?"

He nodded. "It feel bad."

"I can get a splint for it, and we can tie it up." She got to her feet. "I'll go look for a branch or something."

"I'd better go with you." Eric got up slowly, his muscles aching. The night breeze was chilly. "You might have to go a long way to find trees. Besides getting a splint, we can gather some wood to make a fire."

"I go too," Kala said. "Get away from edge of cliff. We make fire somewhere safer."

They walked across the plateau, going down the slope, the rising moon bright enough to light their way until they got to the forest. Eric wished he still had the flashlight he'd taken from the *Kamalo,* but that had been taken from him in Eden. Still they managed to find some dry sticks and leaves, and then found a clearing near a little stream. Eric used the lighter from the *Kamalo* to start a fire. Noelani found a straight green stick to splint Kala's arm.

"But there's nothing to tie it up with," she said, "unless I use my dress."

Eric pulled off his shirt.

"Here," he said tearing it down the front. "You can use part of this for the splint and part for a sling."

Kala bathed his blood-covered arm in the stream.

"It not bleed much now," he told them, "but it feel like fire."

Noelani gently tied the branch to his lower arm.

"This will have to do for now. Maybe it'll feel better when you keep it still."

Eric stared into the leaping flames.

"You'll both have to see a doctor. And I have to get to the ranch to find my dad. I think we'd better go down to the boat, as soon as it's light, and head for Halawa Bay. Then we can hike up to the ranch. They may have a doctor there, but if they don't, they can tell us where to find one."

In the firelight, the snake on Noelani's branded cheek seemed to glisten and writhe. She seemed to have forgotten about it as she made a sling.

"What about your dad? What do you think happened to him?" Noelani questioned.

117

"I don't know. I hope he's okay. I left word at the ranch, so if he contacts the people there, he'll at least know I'm alive."

She glanced across the fire at him. "You mean he thinks you're dead?"

"The last time he saw me, I was falling out of that helicopter." Popoki pushed herself against Eric's knee, and he scratched her head absently. "I'm not even sure that he's alive, either. That's why I've got to get to the ranch. If he's not there yet, I'll call the police again—see what they've found out."

"The police—" Noelani and Kala exchanged nervous glances, and again Eric noticed they seemed to share some secret.

Kala spoke to Noelani.

"Maybe we better talk to police, too. Right?"

"I don't know." She tied the two ends of the sling around his neck, looking worried. "She'll kill us if we try anything against her, Kala."

"C'mon. Tell me what you two are talking about."

Noelani completed the splinting of Kala's arm and sat down by the fire, across from Eric. Kala sat with his back against a tree, his eyes half closed.

"You tell him, Noelani."

"Okay. I think I can trust you, Eric. You know almost everything now anyway. Well, we think there's something strange going on in Eden," she began.

"You bet there's something strange going on. Look what she did to you, and tried to do to me. The police should hear about that."

"I know. But there's something else I saw. I wonder about it many times."

Eric patted the purring cat.

"What was it?"

"Something I saw before I knew about Eden or Pele. It was near the place where my parents died. I only went there to put flowers on the place where they fell—"

"Fell?" Eric was startled. "How did they fall?"

Her voice was small and sad. "They jumped together from a cliff in the forest."

"Why?"

"Because they couldn't be together. Because my mother had royal blood and my father was only from a family of warriors." The firelight made shadows on her face. "I can tell you about it if you want to hear the story."

Eric nodded.

"I didn't even know there was still Hawaiian royalty around."

"Oh, yes. There aren't any kings and queens left now. But there are some who have royal blood. My mother's family never forgets that." She sighed. "Anyway, my mother and grandmother lived in a big house up in the mountains near the ancient temple. Our ancestors have lived in that place for hundreds of years, but they changed the house, you know. Made it better—more modern.

"So my father was hunting near there one day when he saw my mother in the kukui grove. I guess they loved each other right away. After that first time, they met secretly. My mother knew her family would not let them see each other. Then one day they ran off to Maui and got married in a church on the other side of the island."

"Did your grandmother ever find out?"

"Yes. When I was born, my mother and father brought me here to Molokai, to my grandmother's house. I guess they hoped she would forgive my mother and accept their marriage because of me—their baby."

"And did she?" Eric asked her.

"No, she was very angry. My uncles and aunts were angry too. It was even worse when they found out my father had accepted the Christian religion. They said my mother had brought shame on all of them. Then my grandmother told my father he would have to go away, that he could not stay married to my mother. They told him he would have to leave my mother and me and never try to see either of us again."

She poked at the fire with a long stick, a faraway expression in her eyes, as though she could see the events she described in her memory. But she was only a baby then, Eric thought. How could she remember? Probably she'd been told about it, and turned the facts over in her mind many times, like he and Alison did about their own mother who had died when they were only two years old.

"When my mother tried to go with my father," she went on, "the family held her prisoner in the house. But she found a way to escape. Before she left, she wrote me a letter and put it in an envelope with her opal ring and this necklace." She pulled a gold chain from the neck of her red flowered dress and held out the large opal pendant that hung on it. The firelight caught the jewel and made it shimmer as though a shattered rainbow was imprisoned inside it.

"And the ring?" Eric asked. "Is that the one you had to give Kimo when you bribed him?"

"Yes. I hated to do it, but it bought my life." She tucked the pendant inside the neck of her dress. "Anyway, my mother also wrote a note to my grandmother, telling her to take care of me and to give me the jewelry and the letter when I was old enough to understand. After that, she left the house. She must have found my father somehow. Maybe he was waiting for her, or

120

maybe she caught up with him before he could go very far. They stayed together in the rain forest that night, and at sunrise they went to the cliff near Eden. There's a story about that cliff, an old story the people of Molokai tell, about Hiiaka, the sister of the goddess Pele, who fell in love with a mortal man and jumped over that cliff when she found he didn't love her. Maybe that's why my mother and father chose to die together there.''

"They jumped over the cliff?" Eric stared at her, finding it hard to believe people really did things like that. It all sounded so much like an old legend. But then he remembered some of the strange things he'd read in the newspapers back home, and decided that people still died for love nowadays, just as they had for hundreds of years.

"Yes," Noelani said quietly. "Some servants who saw them said they jumped with their arms around each other." She gazed into the crackling fire and shivered in spite of its warmth.

"When I was seven, my grandmother gave me my mother's letter. It said that she and my father loved me very much, and because I had royal blood, I must stay with my grandmother."

"How come you went to boarding school in Honolulu?" Eric asked.

"My grandmother was old. She brought me up, and taught me how to behave like royalty. When I was twelve, she died. There were only servants left in the house then. My aunts and uncles didn't want me, so I was sent to the Kamehameha School. I lived there in Honolulu. Our school choir traveled to the mainland. That's when I met you, Eric, at the White House in Washington. I decided then that I liked you," she said softly. "When I came back to the Islands, I was lonesome for my home island of Molokai, so I ran away from school. I came back here to be near the place where my parents died."

Eric was touched by her story, and by the emotions he could see on her mutilated face. Knowing what he now knew about her, he was even more shocked at what Pele had done to her. He felt protective, outraged, and tender, but how could he tell her what he felt? This seemed to be neither the time nor the place, with Kala sitting impassively against the tree, and the leaping fire between them. And so, instead, he asked, "How did you know the place where your parents died?"

"My grandmother showed it to me. After my mother disappeared from the house, my grandmother told the servants to find her and bring her back. They found the bodies, and took them back to my grandmother. Every year on that day, my grandmother went to the bottom of the cliff to place flowers there. She loved my mother very much. I think she loved my father, too. But she loved her royal ancestors more."

"And she took you to the place?"

"Yes. So I knew where it was." Noelani fingered the gold chain. "The day I came back, I picked hibiscus and ginger blossoms to place there, and plumeria and wood-rose. Then I saw some beautiful flowers in a grove not far away. They were the prettiest orchids I'd ever seen. So I picked some of those to give to the spirits of my parents. After that, I went back to the orchid garden to pick some to put in my hair. I thought they were growing wild."

"But they were the Eden orchids."

"Yes. They grow wild there, but Pele claims them as her own. That day she was nearby and she saw me picking them."

"What did she do?"

"She was angry." Noelani hesitated, looking thoughtful. "At first I believed she was angry about the flowers, but I wonder if it was something else. She and the men with her were working with other plants, a tall plant I didn't recognize. They were taking little leaves from the tops of the plants and putting them into bags. When she saw me watching them, she was very angry. But then she smiled and started to talk to me about how old I was and where I'd come from. When she found out that my grandmother had died and that I was now running away from the school in Honolulu, she invited me to her house and gave me pineapple juice and roast meat and introduced me to the Children of Eden."

"Just like that?"

"Yes. I lived in Eden for two years, and so did Kala. I guess Pele was sort of like a mother to all of us there."

Eric somehow felt responsible. She and Kala had lost their home. No matter how he felt about Pele, those two had been happy in Eden for a while at least.

"So then I came along and got you into trouble," he said.

"No. It isn't your fault. Pele was angry with me before you came here. Every year, without telling her, I go to the place where my parents died, to remember them with flowers. This year I went again, and I saw her again, working with those same plants. Only this time I saw something else. I saw them putting something from those plants around the cords that the orchid leis are twined on."

"But you don't know what the plants are?" Eric was mystified.

"No. But when Pele saw me there, she was furious again. This time she accused me of spying on them. She

123

said the gods would punish me if I ever told anyone about what I'd seen there.''

"Well, why was she so worried if you didn't know what they were doing anyway?"

"I don't know, Eric. Maybe she thought I knew more than I did. Anyway, she told me these were special plants to make decorations for the gods—to hang in the place of the fire. She said only special people had permission to handle those plants."

"But you don't believe that, do you?"

Noelani's voice was beginning to sound sleepy.

"No. Those plants were being used on the leis, not for decorations. I knew that much. So when I got back to Eden, I met Kala and he knew something was bothering me. He questioned me, so I told him about it."

Eric looked over at Kala to ask if he knew anything more, but Kala was stretched out on the ground under the tree, apparently asleep. Eric, too, felt exhausted, but he was curious about the plants Noelani had seen.

"Can you tell me exactly what those plants looked like?"

"They were tall and had thin leaves." Noelani yawned and curled up beside the rocks that ringed the fire.

"And Kala thinks you ought to tell the police about what you saw?"

"Well, we both think it seems strange that Pele got so angry. And what would she think I was telling you in the marketplace, if it wasn't about what I'd seen? Why did she think we were plotting against her? Why did she make this mark on my cheek?" Noelani's voice trailed off into a sleepy murmur.

Eric stretched himself out on his side of the fire, with the cat lying against him. The whole thing seemed strange to him, too. A vague thought ran through his mind, a glimmer of something important that he couldn't name right now. Tomorrow, he thought sleepily. Tomorrow he would remember what he couldn't remember right now.

10 • The Mystery of Eden

Eric jerked involuntarily and sat up. He had been having a nightmare. A giant red spider with legs as huge as tree trunks had been attacking him. He could feel its cold breath and see its colossal jaws opening, spitting saliva at him. Suddenly the spider had two heads and began to attack Alison, his twin. It was awful.

He looked around and discovered he was alone. Noelani and Kala weren't there, and it wasn't even light yet. Where had they gone? For a moment he wondered if he and Popoki were alone in a gray wet world.

The crackling of the underbrush signaled Noelani coming toward him, carrying an armload of firewood. She was followed by Kala.

"You didn't sleep well." The girl bent to drop the wood within the circle of stones. "You were tossing and moaning."

"I was having nightmares."

Eric got up, flexed his stiff legs, and pulled the butane lighter out of his jeans pocket to start the fire.

Kala dropped the bunch of ripe bananas he held in his good arm.

"Breakfast."

Eric helped himself.

"Don't they have any bacon-and-egg trees around here?"

"Lucky to find almost-ripe bananas."

Kala peeled one, having difficulty doing it one-handedly.

"How's the arm?"

"Sore. All of us alive. Not much else matter."

They warmed themselves next to the fire and ate the bananas, while Eric fought the images of juicy sausages, scrambled eggs, and pancakes dripping with syrup. How long ago had it been, anyway? He counted, holding up his fingers, frowning.

"What are you doing?" Noelani laughed.

"Figuring out how long since I ate a square meal. Let's see. It's only two days. This will be my fourth day here in Hawaii. Seems like four weeks."

"Then your dad's been missing for four days, right?"

"As far as I know. Today I want to get to the *Puu O Hoku* Ranch to find out. Is that okay with you two?"

Noelani looked doubtfully toward Kala.

"Not good for us to stay here," Kala said. "Cabin's all gone now. So, we go to ranch. See the doctor. Fix my arm. Maybe fix that burn on Noelani, too. Sure, let's get boat and head for Halawa Bay."

"Well—okay," Noelani hesitated. "But I'm not letting anybody see my face, except maybe a doctor. And I'm not going to tell him how I got this snake scar either."

"Do you still think Pele is some kind of goddess?" Eric impatiently asked Noelani. "You still think she'll kill you if you tell anybody what she did to you?''

Noelani looked stubbornly at the ground, not answering.

"Then what about telling the police? You said last night you might talk to them. Remember those strange plants you told me about? And all the suspicious things you saw?" Suddenly Eric remembered what he hadn't remembered the night before. "What did those plants look like? Tell me again.''

She shrugged.

"They just looked like tall green plants with skinny leaves. Like weeds.''

"Weeds!" Excitement flowed through him. "I'll bet that's what they are, all right. Describe them as well as you can. Carefully.''

A frown of concentration wrinkled her nose.

"Well, they had thin stalks, and the leaves grew out around them in groups of three, I think, bigger at the bottom and smaller at the top.''

"Shiny leaves?''

"No, I'm sure they weren't shiny.''

"Is that all you can remember?''

"Yes.''

"Well," Eric said, "it would make sense, if that's what they were. There's a lot of profit in selling weed.''

"Weed?" Kala and Noelani both looked mystified.

"Grass. Marijuana. I thought everybody knew what marijuana plants look like. You see pictures of them all over the place.''

"Not in Eden," Noelani said.

That made sense too. Eden was a primitive place, Eric knew. Pele must make sure it stayed that way. He'd seen no TV sets or radios. No place for films to be shown. The only magazines and paperbacks he saw were in

Pele's house. The Children of Eden had been kept ignorant of almost everything most kids their age knew about. No wonder Pele was upset to find that copy of *Faces* magazine Noelani had. Noelani must have smuggled it in.

"It all adds up," he told them. "Pele and those special helpers of hers could have been growing marijuana up in the mountain behind Eden where you wouldn't ever know about it."

"We weren't allowed up there," Noelani said. "Nobody had any reason to go there, except me. And Pele didn't know I went every year. I never told her."

"Okay," Eric said. "I know you can make rope out of marijuana. That's what hemp is. So they could twine the orchid blossoms over the hemp to hide it, so they'd look like ordinary orchid leis. Only they cost a lot more than ordinary leis, so most tourists wouldn't be interested in buying them. Didn't you say you had regular customers for those, Noelani?"

"Yes. Usually the same men bought them from me every time. Sometimes they bought two or three of them."

"And the other girls—did they have regular customers for the expensive leis too?"

"Sure. We used to laugh about those men who bought them, how they must have more than one girl they were buying for."

"Those men must be pushers. They could package little pieces of the rope and sell them on the street. Probably they'd make four or five times as much on those packages as they paid for the whole orchid lei."

Noelani looked doubtful.

"But suppose just a regular person bought one of them? Wouldn't that give it all away?"

"Chances are he wouldn't discover the string of the lei was made from marijuana. Why would he even look at it? After the orchids faded, he'd likely throw it away. Even if he did find out, how could he trace you? Didn't you say the girls of Eden who sold the leis went to different places every week?"

"That's true. We did. And Pele could radio to those special customers to tell them when we'd be in their city, and where we'd be selling the leis. Sometimes it was an airport, or a shopping center, or any place where a lot of people would be. Different places all the time."

There was realization, now, on her beautiful scarred face.

"So that's why Pele was so angry when I gave one of the special leis to you. She was afraid I knew what the plants were, or that you would know. She may even have thought I was giving it to you so you'd send the police to Eden."

"Right. So she thought that by scarring your face and telling you lies, you'd be too afraid to do anything about it. And that's why she tried to kill me." Eric rubbed his forehead thoughtfully. "She must feel really frightened now that both Kala and I escaped. But then, she isn't sure we did escape, is she? She might believe Kala and I drowned in the bay, and she thinks Kimo pushed you out in the ocean, too."

The girl's eyes seemed to darken, to close out this thought.

"Pele knows. She will chase us with wind and fire and earthquakes until we are all destroyed."

Eric turned his head to hide his anger at the hold Pele had on his friends.

The sun was rising to light up the world, but nothing he could say seemed to cast any light on the dark superstition that Pele had thrown over the minds of his two friends. He heard a rustle close by, and saw that Popoki had caught herself a small rodent for breakfast.

Noelani was looking beseechingly at him.

"You don't believe Pele will chase us, do you, Eric? Kala and I have seen many things. We know this is true. We know Pele is the volcano goddess who's come back again. She can destroy us all, and she will, just as she promised."

Eric looked at Kala. "You still think that way, too?"

Kala grinned, unexpectedly. "We better put out fire now and sail for Halawa Bay. Sun's coming up. Rain will stop soon." He poked a long stick at the fire, separating the burning logs.

Eric persisted.

"You haven't changed your mind about telling the police, have you? Pele's got to be stopped before someone else gets killed or—mutilated. When we get to the ranch, we can talk to my dad about it. He'll know how to get hold of the right people, like the Drug Enforcement Agency or somebody. They can go out to Eden and break up Pele's drug ring."

"But we're not even sure it is a drug ring," Noelani protested.

"Well, it all makes sense, doesn't it? It seems to be the only explanation. But okay, just suppose Pele's not selling marijuana. Suppose she's just doing what she says—taking care of a colony of young people to start a new world when the gods destroy the rest of the Hawaiian Islands. Then why are the gods taking so long? You've both lived in Eden for two years. Why is it taking them two years and more?" He looked from one to the other.

Kala shrugged indifferently, but Noelani answered.

131

"Nobody knows when the destruction will come. Only the gods. But it will be soon."

Eric knew there was no reasoning with an answer like that. He tried another argument.

"Okay, if Pele could really find us and kill us, why hasn't she done it by now?" As he spoke, he felt another tremor of the earth, brief and fleeting.

Noelani must have felt it too, for her eyes held fear.

"Maybe we won't get to Halawa Bay alive," she said.

There was nothing further to say. Eric helped Kala scatter the fire and throw dirt on the parts that still burned. Then they headed for the stream they'd followed before. The sun was over the edge of the eastern cliff when they began their hike beside the stream down to the place where they'd beached the catamaran. They went single file down the goat trail, Popoki coming along behind them. As Kala had predicted, the rain had stopped, but had left a rainbow in memory of its passing. A flock of white terns flew along its edge. At this distance, it seemed to Eric they were sliding down the curve of color that arched across the sky.

They walked silently. Ohia leaves made filigree shadows on the flat rocks. Ti plants, nibbled by goats, grew in clumps beside the stream, and on its other side, where the cliff rose, Eric could see tiny droplets of water sparkling like diamonds on moss and fern that sprang from the crevices. Everything was a shade of green, so that he felt he walked through part of the rainbow's spectrum, drenched in emerald and turquoise, olive and aquamarine, chartreuse and jade.

When they rounded a bend, he saw two high waterfalls dropping from a plateau, sliding down the verdant slope, bouncing outward where the cliff leaned back, catching the wind and sheeting across the slope, the spray reflecting the light in thousands of rainbows. His breath caught in his throat. It was so beautiful, this island. Beautiful and terrifying at the same time. Like Noelani, it was loveliness marred by a frightening scar, and as far as Eric was concerned, that scar on Molokai was Pele. The more he learned about her, the more horrifying she became. He had to convince Noelani and Kala to tell the police what they knew. If they didn't—

As they walked, the day grew warmer. Soon they came to a place where the stream formed a pool, edged by fragrant white ginger blossoms that hung over the water. Noelani stopped here, started to walk on, then turned back.

"I'd like to wash myself," she said. "I'm hot and sticky and dirty, and the water looks so good."

Eric and Kala went to wait in a little clearing where climbing pananus twisted around kukui trees. Popoki went with them to curl up and nap until they were ready to go on. When Noelani found them, she looked fresh and lovely. Even her wet dress hung gracefully from her shoulders. She had twisted a spray of the ginger in her hair. The comparison was too much for Eric and Kala. They left her with the cat while they headed for the pool.

The cold water felt good against Eric's forehead, where the cut was still sore. He and Kala undressed and washed in the pool.

"No *mo'o* here," Kala said happily. He pronounced the word *moh-oh*.

"Who's *mo'o*?"

"Evil water spirits. They hide in mountain pools. Deep ones. This one not deep enough for them."

Eric wondered if he was serious. Kala smiled so seldom it was hard to tell.

"Are they anything like mermaids?" he asked.

133

"Mermaids only superstition."

Kala ducked under the water with a splash.

When he came up again, Eric said, "When you got me out of that shed in Eden, Kala, you could have just dropped me off along the coast somewhere instead of bringing me up here. Why did you want me to see Noelani?"

"You her friend."

Kala had taken off his sling, and now he gingerly splashed water over his injured arm, then climbed out to the bank.

"But it was more than that, wasn't it?" Eric got out, too, and began pulling on his jeans. "Was it because you thought I could talk her into seeing a doctor?"

"For sure. I've no money to help her. I know nobody. You can take her to best doctors. They fix her face. Make her feel beautiful again."

Eric wondered at his choice of words. "Make her *feel* beautiful again." He hadn't said, "Make her *look* beautiful again." Could it be that Kala didn't care how Noelani looked with a scar on her face, but only how she felt?

For a moment he was struck by the difference in their reactions to the disfiguring burn. Eric had wondered if he could ever feel at ease in going places now with Noelani, as he had hoped to do. Eric was concerned about her looking good. Kala only seemed to want her to feel good about herself. Which one of them was the better friend, Eric had to ask himself.

But then, he reasoned, my situation is different from Kala's. I'm used to dating many pretty girls. Maybe Kala's never cared for any other girl. And I live in a different environment, where how your dates *look* is more important sometimes than what they are really like.

134

Kala, here on this island, wouldn't have friends or family around to ask questions or embarrass a girl with a scarred face. I would want to take her to meet my friends at parties, and take her to good restaurants—even to the White House, maybe. Kala would probably only take her out sailing or fishing.

After thinking over these differences, Eric realized something that hadn't been obvious to him before. Suddenly he said out loud to Kala, "Do you love Noelani?"

A strange look came over Kala's face before he composed it into an expression of calm indifference.

"Noelani has royal blood. I got nobody, no money, nothing. My father was fisherman before he die. My mother was waitress. She on mainland now with my little brothers and sisters."

He lifted his chin proudly.

"I got nothing much, but I can work. I build boat. I learn to do many things. I can earn money to help Noelani—to pay for what she needs. Except maybe doctor. That costs a lot. So I bring you here because she need you. I stay with her as long as she want me."

He finished dressing and turned to go back to the grove where Noelani waited.

Eric followed, thinking about the strange situation they were in. Each of them loved Noelani in his own way. If it ever came to a choice, which would Noelani prefer?

11 • *The Disappearance of Dr. Thorne*

The little catamaran waited where they had left it high on the rocky beach, undamaged by the earthquakes. Before launching it, Eric, Noelani, and Kala pried a mid-morning snack of *opihi* off the rocks by the ocean and shared some with Popoki. Eric felt he was getting to be expert at living off the land as he dug the limpets out of their shells and swallowed them. He saved some to use as bait, remembering that Kala had a fishing pole on board, and he had extra hooks in his pocket.

The three of them got the boat on the water, and Eric set up the mast and ran up the sail, while Noelani carried the cat on board. They sailed out of the inlet, blown by soft trade winds over a calm sea. Gliding smoothly along the folded green cliffs that edged the coast, they headed east toward Halawa Bay.

Kala managed the tiller with his sound left hand, saying he needed no help. Eric baited a hook with *opihi* and trailed the line in the water. Noelani sat on the deck with Eric and told him about Molokai.

"They used to call this the Forgotten Island, maybe because the leper colony is here, or maybe because a long time ago it had such powerful, fierce *kahunas* that everyone stayed away from them."

"What's a *kahuna,* anyway?"

"A priest of the gods. The ones here on Molokai used to put people to death for almost any reason at all."

"Sounds like Pele," Eric said. "But now they call this the Friendly Island. Right?"

She nodded.

"It even looks friendly today, doesn't it? Usually it rains along this coast."

"I know. I've seen a lot of this coast in the last few days!" Eric felt a tug at his line and pulled it in. It was empty. He baited it again and dropped it into the water. "Hope I can catch a big fish for lunch."

After a while he gave up trying. Kala was heading the boat into a wide bay.

"Is this Halawa?" Eric asked.

"For sure."

"Then we'll have lunch at the ranch!" Eric didn't notice that his friends did not share his enthusiasm.

The bay was less rocky and more accessible than the others they'd landed in. With the catamaran safe on the pebbly shore, Kala pointed to a wide trail that led up the slope to the high plateau above.

"We can follow that. Takes us to *Puu O Hoku* Ranch."

Eric forgot his hunger in his eagerness to reach their destination. He led the way up the trail that was rutted with tire tracks. As they went, he found himself walking faster until he was almost running. His companions had to ask him to slow down.

"I guess I'm impatient to see my father!" Eric explained. He refused to think of the alternative. Of course the hijackers would have let Dad and the pilot go without hurting them. What good would it do them to commit any more crimes? All they wanted, anyway, was an escape from the island.

Thinking about the hijackers made him remember that one of them had taken the orchid lei from him in the helicopter. It was a long shot, but could it be they had some connection with Pele? Suppose those men knew the orchid leis were strung on marijuana? Suppose they'd been told by Pele to get the evidence away from him, because she knew about Eric's meeting with Noelani. Maybe they were some of Pele's men who watched the girls from Eden while they sold their leis. If they were, they'd feel they had to get the evidence away from him before he took it to the police.

Eric stopped on the trail and waited for Kala and Noelani to catch up. When they did, he told them what he'd been thinking.

Kala didn't believe it could be true.

"You mean they know where you go, follow and get in copter with you just to get lei?"

"Sure." Eric answered walking more slowly now. "I don't think they could have carried it off if Diamond Head hadn't started blowing its top that day. But in all that excitement, they had a perfect excuse to get into the helicopter with us without anybody guessing they were really after the orchids."

"But isn't hijacking as big a crime, if not bigger, than selling dope?" Noelani objected.

"I'm not sure," Eric said. "In an emergency, maybe crowding into a private helicopter could be excused. But I think they'd do anything to keep the police from finding out about the marijuana. That's a big business.

138

Pele and her helpers are probably making loads of money. That's why they were so afraid we'd stop it, Noelani. And Pele was ready to commit murder for it."

Noelani grew pale, and the brand on her cheek turned an angry red. Her voice sounded angry too. "You don't know if it's true or not, Eric. You're just guessing. You could be wrong."

"Sure. But you've got to admit that everything makes a lot of sense if you look at it my way."

As they picked up their pace, they lapsed into an uncomfortable silence. Soon the slopes around them were open fields where they could see cattle grazing. When they finally reached the plateau, they began to see cars and people around the lodge ahead of them. Eric started to think of things like hot showers, good meals, and clean clothes.

Noelani and Kala were hanging back. Finally Noelani stopped.

"I—I can't go in there, Eric. Not with all those people."

Eric understood. After his own first reaction to the brand on her face, he'd almost forgotten it was there, but other people might stare and ask questions.

"But I've got to see my dad," he said. "I've got to let him know I'm alive. And I want him to meet both of you." He looked at Kala, bare chested and barefoot, his jeans torn and dirty, and he knew he must look the same. "Don't worry, Noelani," he said, "everyone will stare at Kala and me, so they'll never notice. We're not exactly dressed for dinner. Come on, let's all go in together."

Noelani still refused.

"I'd be too nervous, with all those people. Anyway, somebody has to stay here with Popoki. They won't want her in the hotel."

"We wait here," Kala said. "You go see your dad. Come back and tell us about it." He sat down on the grass under a tree, and Noelani picked up Popoki and sat down beside him.

"Okay," Eric said. "I'll be back soon."

He felt conspicuous himself, now, barefoot and wearing only jeans. He passed several people in front of the lodge, but they paid little attention to him. Once inside the building, he could see why. It was large and rustic, radiating an atmosphere of comfortable hominess. Many of the guests seemed to be here for hunting and fishing, judging by their casual clothing. Eric went to the front desk and spoke to the white-haired man who stood behind it.

"My name is Eric Thorne. I'd like to see my father, Dr. Randall Thorne, who's staying here."

The man looked worried.

"Dr. Thorne hasn't checked in yet. The IAF people asked us to keep a suite for him, but they tell us he's still missing. The police are conducting a search for him."

The news hit Eric in the stomach. He hadn't dared let himself think that his father might have disappeared. Now he was faced with it. Dizzily, he gripped the edge of the desk.

"Are you all right, Mr. Thorne?"

Eric managed to force the words between his dry lips.

"Yes. It's just that I thought—"

"I'm sorry. I thought you were aware of the situation. The police and the IAF are doing everything they can, I know." The man rang a little bell, and in a moment a tall young man came through a doorway behind him. The older man spoke to him softly, then addressed Eric again. "Are you sure you're all right?"

"Yes." Eric managed to straighten himself and let go

of the desk, but he knew he must look the way he felt, shaken and worried.

"If you would like, my assistant will show you to the rooms reserved for Dr. Thorne. As I said, the IAF asked us to keep the suite ready for his arrival."

Eric tried to stop his thoughts from whirling long enough to understand what the man was saying. His father had reserved a suite of rooms here. He could use the room phone now to call the police and find out what they knew about his dad.

The man's comments seeped in slowly, so that it was a moment before Eric answered. "Yes. Yes, of course, I will go to the rooms and wait for news of my father there."

The assistant took a key from the pigeonhole and came around the desk. As Eric started to follow him he remembered Noelani and Kala. "I have some friends outside."

"Would you like me to send someone to bring them here?"

"No. Just give me the key and I'll get them, myself."

The man at the desk spoke with concern. "If you need anything, please let us know."

"Thank you," Eric said, gratefully.

He went back outside and walked the short distance to Noelani and Kala, waiting under the tree. They seemed to know by his expression that something was wrong before he told them the horrible news.

"But there's good news too," he went on, "there's a suite of rooms that Dad reserved. We can go there to call the police. The man said it was okay for us to stay there."

Noelani shook her head stubbornly.

"No. I'm not going in there. I'm sorry about your

father, Eric, and I know you have to find out everything you can about him, but I'm not going to face all those people. Not looking like this.''

"We come all this way to find doctor, too," Kala reminded her. "Now you gonna hide from doctor?"

Noelani looked scared and confused.

"We find out." Kala stood up and reached out for Noelani's hand to pull her to her feet. "Maybe you no want one, but I do. My arm hurt like fire."

The girl refused to give him her hand.

"What about Popoki? We can't take her in there."

Eric had an idea.

"We can take her to the back door, or wherever the kitchen might be. We'll find out. We can ask the people there if they'll feed her table scraps. She'll wait around outside for us as long as she has food and she knows we're inside."

"Okay, then I'll wait here with her. You go find out first."

No amount of arguing could move her, so finally Eric and Kala went to find the kitchen.

At the back of the lodge, they saw two young girls, about ten years old, playing with a ball. On impulse, Eric spoke to them. "You girls like cats?"

They stopped their play and stared from him to Kala with questioning eyes. Then one of them smiled at him.

"Sure. Why?"

"I just wondered. Do you live here in the lodge?"

She shook her head and pointed across the fields.

"No. Over there. My mother works here."

"And you stay here and play while she's at work?"

They both nodded and the other girl said, "Only till school starts. Then we go to school."

"Would you do us a favor and look after our cat for a

142

few days?'' he asked them. ''We're staying in the lodge and we can't take the cat inside with us. If you'll keep an eye on her when you're here, I'll—'' he started to say he'd pay them, but did he have any money? Did he even still have his wallet, or had he lost it somewhere along the way? He dug into his jeans pocket, found it, and sighed with relief. ''I'll give you each a dollar,'' he said.

The girls looked at each other, then back to him, and both of them said ''yes'' at once.

''Where's the cat?'' the taller girl asked him.

''Come on. I'll show you.''

Eric and Kala led the way down the road and the two girls followed them. Noelani saw them coming and waited, stiff and anxious. As soon as the little girls saw the cat curled up in her lap, they ran ahead to pet her.

''What's her name?'' one of them asked Noelani.

''Popoki.''

The girls laughed. ''That's a funny name. It just means *cat*.'' The girl who spoke looked up at Noelani, and her laughter stopped short as she stared at her face. Eric caught his breath as she asked, ''What's that mark on your cheek?''

Noelani's face reddened. ''It's a—scar.''

The other girl reached out to touch it with her finger. ''It looks like a snake.''

Noelani pulled away from her touch, and for a moment there was an embarrassed, painful silence as Eric tried to think of something to do or say that would relieve the tension.

But the two little girls had already turned their attention back to the cat.

''Come on, Popoki, you can come and play ball with us, and we'll get you some food.'' One child picked her up, and Popoki offered no resistance.

"Is there a back door into the lodge?" Eric asked the two girls.

They nodded.

Eric spoke to Noelani. "Will you come in the lodge now? We can go in the back way without meeting anybody."

Noelani got to her feet and followed them down the road toward the lodge. Eric silently thanked his new friends. Maybe Noelani had expected more of a reaction than she got from them. It might have been exactly what she needed to have them react the way they did.

There was nobody around when they entered the back door, and they found a stairway that was deserted. Noelani glanced around, but gave no other sign of anxiety. They went up the stairs without speaking.

As they walked down the hallway on the second floor, a man came out of a door and walked in their direction. Eric and Kala were on either side of Noelani. She held her head high and looked straight ahead. Whether it was because of the hall or the man's preoccupation with his own affairs, he passed with only a glance at them, and Eric could have shouted with joy. Noelani kept her composure until he pulled out the key and let them into his father's suite. Then she sank onto the nearest couch and put her face in her hands. Eric could see she was shaking.

"It wasn't all that bad, was it?" he asked her gently.

It was a moment before she took her hands away and looked up at him.

"No," she said, "but I was scared."

Kala grunted. "We gotta get a doctor."

"First I've got to talk to the police." Eric headed for the telephone he could see on a low table by the bed. "I've got to find out about Dad."

144

It was a few minutes before the hotel operator could put him through to the police in Kaunakakai, and another wait before he found someone who knew about his father. At last the call went through. Captain Kona remembered his conversation with Eric several days ago. He sounded optimistic, although his news wasn't good.

"We know the helicopter is down, but we're not sure where. We're searching for it now. It was spotted in the vicinity of Lanai."

"Lanai? That's not far from Molokai, is it?"

"No, but we've searched the island and haven't found it yet."

"How long ago was it seen?"

"Yesterday, heading for Lanai. But the day before that, we had a report that it was on Maui. I'm afraid we just don't know where it is, and with this emergency situation on Oahu, we're working shorthanded."

Eric's hopes sank.

"Isn't there something I can do to help?"

"Not a thing." Captain Kona paused, and Eric could hear busy voices in the background. "We're expecting to have news for you very shortly, though. Just leave me your number and I'll contact you as soon as we know anything. The best thing you can do is wait and let us handle it."

Eric gave the captain his phone number, and after he'd hung up, feeling helpless, he told the others what the captain had said.

"Hang loose," Kala said to him. "Your dad is a smart man. He gonna be okay. Police will find him for sure."

"But they haven't found the copter yet, and it's been four days!" Eric paced the floor restlessly.

"There lots of places to hide copter on islands. It be here someplace. Police find it." Kala seemed confident, and somehow that made Eric feel a little better. He stopped his pacing.

"I guess there's no use worrying," he said, as he picked up the phone again. "I'll see if we can find a doctor."

There was a doctor at the lodge, he learned, and both Kala and Noelani could see him right away.

After discovering that Kala's arm wasn't broken, only badly bruised, the doctor took off the splint and replaced the makeshift sling.

Then he examined Noelani's face.

"Hmmm. Cauterized right down through the epidermis," he muttered, shaking his head. "How did it happen?"

Noelani's answer was almost a whisper. "It's a burn."

"I can see that, young lady. Now, would you mind telling me who did it to you?"

Noelani would only shake her head.

The doctor spoke to Kala and Eric. "If you know who did this, I'd suggest you report them to the police," he said curtly. "As for treating it, the burn is already healing. There isn't much more I can do. But as you can see, it's leaving a nasty scar.

"Plastic surgery might help, I can't say for sure. I'm not qualified as a plastic surgeon. There are several here in the Islands. I can give you their names and addresses. And I'd suggest you see one immediately."

He wrote several names on a piece of paper, and Eric saw that the addresses were all on the islands of Oahu and Hawaii. He wanted to ask the doctor what the plastic surgeons could do—if they could remove the scar from Noelani's face, but she seemed anxious to leave. On the way back to his father's suite, he could see she was upset.

146

"One thing I'm sure of," he said as he opened the door. "I'm going to take the doctor's advice and report Pele to the police. I don't care whether you agree or not."

Noelani sat on the couch, looking pale and shaken, while Kala took a chair.

"No," she said to Eric. "Don't. They can't do anything to Pele. Nobody can. She'll destroy all of us first."

"That wrong!" Kala cried out. He stood up suddenly, and Eric saw that his usually placid face was twisted with anger. "She try to wreck your life and mine, Noelani. We gotta stop her!"

Something had changed in Kala. The girl looked at him, surprised.

"But you know the powers she has as well as I do."

He shook his head violently, his dark hair falling across his broad forehead. Eric realized for the first time how handsome he really was.

"No. She tell us lies. She tell everyone lies. She try to run our lives the way she want."

Noelani was angry now.

"She was like a mother to me for two years, Kala, and to you, too. We had no home but Eden—no mother but Pele. We can't just turn against her like this."

His voice softened, but he was still angry.

"*Your* mother never burn you like that. *My* mother never burn me like that. Pele did. She try to kill Eric. She hurt anybody stand in her way. She not love you or me like our mothers. She only love power. She keep us poor and stupid so we obey her." He turned, strode across the room and glared out the window.

"How can you talk that way?" Noelani seemed shocked.

"Because I just begin to get smart." Kala turned to

147

face her again. "Other people, like Eric, they free people—do what they like, go where they want. You and me, we work for Pele, do what Pele want, go where Pele want us to go. She says she has *mana* like goddess, but I don't believe that, not any more. Only when we are afraid, we do what she want." He paused and lifted his head, speaking firmly. "I not afraid no more."

Eric was stunned. He could hardly believe this was the same easygoing Kala he'd known for the past few days. He wanted to clap him on the back and congratulate him. It couldn't be easy for him to go against all the brainwashing Pele had done, as well as Noelani's obvious disapproval. Eric stayed quiet in his chair beside the phone, feeling he shouldn't interrupt. This was between Kala and Noelani. It didn't matter how Eric felt at this moment. It was the two Children of Eden who had to decide how they felt. He watched Noelani look at Kala with disbelieving eyes.

"So you think we should report her to the police?"

Kala nodded.

"If you still afraid of her, think what more can she do to you? She already try to destroy your beauty. She tell Kimo to drop you in ocean. She already do worst she could to you. What you afraid of now?"

For a moment Noelani stared at him, her eyes dark with disillusionment, as though this thought had not occurred to her. Then she lay her head against her arm on the end of the couch, and sobbed.

Kala and Eric watched helplessly as the torrent of tears subsided and she looked up at Kala again.

"I guess I want to believe she's a goddess, Kala. I guess I want to believe she's right and powerful. Because if she isn't—she must be some kind of monster." She began to cry again, softly this time.

Kala turned to Eric.

"Call police, please," he said firmly.

Eric yearned to go to Noelani, put his arms around her, to comfort her. Instead he lifted the phone and spoke to the hotel operator. "Get me the police again, please."

Captain Kona was not there this time, so Eric's call was transferred to Sergeant Lee.

The sergeant told Eric that he knew about Pele and Eden, and had had other complaints about them. Eric told him everything, about his arrival in Eden, the threatened death by fire, and Noelani's branding. Then he spoke about the plants Noelani had seen, and the leis she sold.

Sergeant Lee seemed very interested.

"But what evidence do you have?" he asked.

"Evidence? What evidence do you want?"

"We need to see the girl's face, find what she was branded with. We need one of the orchid leis. Some of the plants. Anything that will prove the charges you're making against this woman."

Eric felt frustrated.

"But we don't have any of those things here with us. We had to leave Eden. Can't you go there yourselves and get the evidence?"

"We've been to Eden before and found nothing wrong there. We have no way of finding evidence unless we know what to look for and where to look for it. If someone familiar with the place can show us, we can do something about it."

"You mean if we show you the plants you'd be able to arrest Pele?"

"Right." Sergeant Lee sounded enthusiastic. "We can send a police helicopter over to Eden to meet you. You can show us where the plants are. Then we'll have something to work on.''

Eric didn't even like to think about returning to Eden.

''Are you sure that's the only way you can do anything?''

''Absolutely sure.''

''Hold on a minute, will you, Sergeant?'' Eric put his hand over the phone's mouthpiece and spoke to his friends. ''He wants us to go back to Eden and show him the evidence.''

Noelani, her eyes still wet with tears, stared at him. Kala's mouth dropped open. Eric knew they were thinking the same thing he was.

To return to Eden was to invite death.

12 • Journey Toward Terror

"My friends and I will have to think about that," Eric told Sergeant Lee. "None of us wants to go back to Eden. But we'll talk it over. I'll call you back when we've decided what to do."

"Well—all right." The sergeant sounded reluctant to let Eric break their phone connection. "We've been trying to find out what's going on in that place for a long time now. A few strange things have happened, and we've heard a lot of stories, but we couldn't get any proof of any crimes. You'll be doing the police and everyone else a favor if you help us stop this woman."

"Yeah, I understand that," Eric said. "But the thing is, we aren't exactly welcome there. It'd be pretty risky."

"I told you," the sergeant pointed out with a touch of impatience, "we'll meet you there. All you have to do is show us some proof. Anyone can make charges against anyone else, you know. You can tell me about this girl's branded face and marijuana and illegal leis all you want, but we can't do a thing without evidence."

"But if we all could go together, we'd feel a lot safer," Eric said. "How about taking us there?"

There was a pause, then, "You're at the *Puu O Hoku* Ranch right now?"

"Yes."

"Let me explain. To pick you up would mean sending a boat there for you. If we cruise into Eden with a boat, Pele's going to have time to make sure there's no evidence left. She'll see us coming and destroy it all while we're still trying to get up the side of that mountain."

The sergeant's voice was patient but firm, and Eric began to get the picture. "And another thing—we can't get a search warrant without some solid facts to go on, so she can refuse to let us set foot in Eden." He laughed bitterly. "She's got a nice little setup there, all privately owned and everything. We can't any more walk into it without a warrant than we can walk into somebody's house. So that means we'll have to go by air; take a helicopter and land up above Eden under cover of the rain forest, and try to keep out of sight until we've got the evidence in our hands. You said the marijuana's growing up there, didn't you?"

"Yeah."

"Okay. And you say there are three of you. There's no room in any of the copters we have available for more than two passengers."

Eric got the point. "So we're right back where we started. We have to get to Eden on our own and meet you there."

"Sorry. I'm afraid so."

"When do you want to go?"

"We-e-e-ll," the sergeant paused, as though checking his schedule. "It's nearly five o'clock now. How about first thing in the morning? Say about seven?"

Eric glanced at Noelani and Kala, who were obviously trying to decipher what was being said from Eric's end of the conversation.

"I'll have to call you back, Sergeant. I can't say whether we'll go or not. We have to talk it over."

Again the sergeant sounded reluctant, but he agreed, and Eric hung up the phone.

"Rats!" he said, disgusted. "I think we've opened up a can of worms."

The other two stared at him, not understanding the expression, so Eric explained, repeating what the sergeant had told him. When he was through, Noelani and Kala both looked as doubtful as he felt.

Kala leaned back in his chair and rubbed his bruised arm with an expression of discouragement.

"Police not go with us?"

"No," Eric said, "but Sergeant Lee is sure anxious for us to go there and get them the evidence. He told me they've been trying to get something on Pele for a long time now."

"Okay," Kala said. "Then we go."

"You really would go back there?" Eric found that hard to believe.

Kala shrugged. "We do what we have to do."

Eric wished he could feel that way. He never wanted to see Pele again, and the idea of trying to get into Eden without bumping into her or one of her followers seemed impossible. Still, he'd been the one who'd wanted to tell the police about her in the first place. He couldn't back down now.

"Okay," he said slowly. "If you're willing to go, I am. How about you, Noelani?"

She seemed apprehensive, listening to them. Now she shook her head emphatically. "I don't want to go."

Kala shrugged as though he'd expected her answer.

"Okay. Stay here. We come back for you."

"No, wait a minute," Eric objected. "You can't stay behind, Noelani. You're the only one who knows exactly where the marijuana grows. And you can show the police your scar and lead them to the bracelet that made it. Kala and I can't do any of that."

"But I don't want to go back there. I'm scared."

Eric could see the terror in her eyes, and his heart melted. He couldn't put her through any more torture.

"All right," he said gently. "You stay here then. Kala and I will go. Just tell us as much as you can about where we can find the plants. At least the police will have that much proof."

She looked relieved. "I'll draw you a map."

"Great."

They found paper and pens in the desk, and Noelani sketched out a rough drawing for them, putting in all the landmarks she could remember. Kala seemed to think he could find it. When she was through, and he'd tucked the folded map in his pocket, Eric went to the phone again and ordered a dinner sent up to them.

"We're going to need all the strength we can get," he told them, "and besides, I'm starving for a good steak."

"Me, too," Noelani said happily, but then she looked doubtful. "How are we going to pay for it, Eric?"

"Just like the doctor's bill. We'll charge it to my dad. He's working for the IAF, and they're paying the bill for this suite. They'll add it all to his expense account, and he'll settle with his office for any extras. Don't worry. I'm sure if he were here, he'd want us to do just what we're doing."

While they waited for the food to be brought to them, Eric and Kala decided they wouldn't wait until morning.

They'd leave the ranch right after dinner so they'd arrive at Eden as soon as it was dark. That way they felt they could climb the cliff with less chance of being seen. When Eric called Sergeant Lee to tell him of their decision, they decided on their meeting place. It would be at the foot of the cliff where Noelani's parents had died.

At six o'clock, while they were still eating their dinner, there was a loud knocking at their door. Eric was so startled he dropped his fork with a clatter.

"Who could that be? Nobody knows we're here."

"Pele?" Noelani whispered, wide-eyed.

Eric started to get up from his chair, but now he hesitated.

"She wouldn't come here," he said, then wondered if that were true. Maybe she would. Maybe she'd found them and was here to finish them off.

He noticed that Kala was darting anxious glances toward the door. While Eric tried to decide what to do, the knock sounded again, and this time he went to answer it. If Pele was there, let her come in and face them. But he could feel his heart racing as he cautiously turned the knob and opened the door a crack.

There stood two little girls, one of them holding Popoki.

With a sigh of relief, Eric opened the door wide.

"Here's your cat," the taller one said, "could we have our money now?"

Smiling, Eric dug into his wallet, pulled out two bills, and handed them one each. "We'll be back tomorrow if you need cat-sitters again," they offered.

"Thanks," Eric answered. "Sorry I forgot to go downstairs to pay you and get the cat, like I promised. Thanks for taking good care of her."

Popoki sniffed the room cautiously until she saw Noelani and Kala, then ran to them.

Eric sat down at the table again. He poked thoughtfully at the baked potato on his plate. "You know something? I just realized that as long as Pele is free, we're going to be scared of our own shadows—like we were when we heard that knock on the door. We'd better eat up and get going, Kala. Every minute we wait only makes us more afraid."

The Hawaiians said nothing, but quickly finished eating their food and set a plate of scraps on the floor for the cat.

When Kala and Eric were ready to go, Noelani went to the door with them.

"If the police phone about my dad, tell them I'll be back as soon as I can," Eric said. "And you can have food sent up here whenever you want. I know Dad would say it was okay."

She nodded, looking sad. "Be careful," she said, and then, as her arms went around his neck and her lips brushed his, Eric hated to let her go. But Kala stood waiting.

Then Noelani kissed Kala, too. Eric felt a tinge of jealousy. Wasn't that a switch, he thought, as he and Kala went down the hall to the back stairway. Eric Thorne, who had every pretty girl in Ivy, Illinois, at his beck and call, and now he had flipped over a girl with a disfigured face. Sure, it had been her beautiful face that had attracted him in the first place, but now it was more than that. She was a sweet and gentle person—and brave too. Noelani would be beautiful, Eric decided, even if plastic surgeons couldn't remove that scar.

Outside the lodge, the two hurried toward the road that would take them to the catamaran down on the beach. They walked in silence, each occupied with his own thoughts—and fear of going to Eden again.

They had left the lodge far behind when they heard a shout behind them. Someone was calling their names. They turned. A girl was running toward them, still a distance away—a girl in a red flowered dress with something white in her arms.

"Noelani!"

They waited until she reached them, out of breath from her race down the road, the cat squirming in her arms.

"I can't do it," she panted. "I can't wait there, worrying about both of you. I'd go crazy wondering what was happening. Take me with you."

Eric didn't know whether to feel happy or angry.

"You know it's going to be dangerous. We might meet Pele again."

"I know. But the police are going to be there to protect us, aren't they?"

"Not until morning. We'll be there tonight." She had obviously made up her mind.

"I thought it over after you left, and decided I was being stupid. I'd have to hide in that room with nothing to do but bite my fingernails until I knew you were safe again, imagining all sorts of things. So I talked myself out of being afraid any more. You were both right. My own fears are worse than anything Pele can do."

She smiled at Eric. "Besides, Popoki was howling. She wanted to come with you, too."

Eric eyed the cat.

"Sure, that's just what we need. White cats show up great in the dark. Let's hope nobody steps on her tail or we've had it."

But he was glad Noelani had the courage to handle her

fear. It felt good to have her with them again.

Kala laughed as Popoki rubbed against Eric's leg.

"That cat been through everything with us already. No use leaving her behind now. She good luck for us."

"We need all the luck we can get." Eric turned, and they all continued down the trail.

Nearing the spot where they'd left the catamaran, they felt another quake. The tremor wasn't as violent as some of the others had been, but it shook the trees and churned the turquoise waters of Halawa Bay. Wouldn't these aftershocks ever stop, Eric wondered, as he steadied himself on the quivering ground. Were these all connected to the eruption of Diamond Head, something like fifty miles away, or was the earth getting ready for another catastrophe?

He heard Noelani's startled cry behind him and turned, wondering if she and Kala still believed Pele was sending the quakes. From their expressions, he thought maybe they did, but they went on, saying nothing. The tremor lasted only a few seconds. When they reached the shore, they saw that the waters of the bay were dark with the rocks and debris that boiled upward from the sea bottom.

Kala hesitated on a high rock by the shore, gazing at the ocean, shaking his head.

"Not looking good," he muttered.

"What is it?" Eric asked him.

"Tide coming up too high."

"Maybe it's just because of that tremor. Maybe it upset the balance of the tides, or something." Eric wasn't sure of what he was saying, but it sounded reasonable. The quake would affect the ocean as well as the land. "It should die down now that the aftershock's stopped."

Kala didn't indicate whether he agreed with Eric or not. He was hurrying to the place where they'd left the catamaran, and Eric could see why he wasn't wasting time. The water was already lapping at the log pontoons when they reached it. There was no need to haul it to the water this time.

Noelani scooped up the cat and stepped on board, with Kala and Eric behind her. Together they raised the mast and, as the water swirled and lifted them, they paddled out to the center of the bay, then hoisted the sail. The sea here had a strong, fishy odor Eric hadn't noticed before, but there was no time to wonder. The sun was low on the horizon. They had to travel as far as they could while it was still light.

There was no friendly chatter this time as they sailed out of the bay and turned westward, toward Eden. Each of them was tense at the thought of what was to come, each of them watched anxiously as they moved past the velvety green cliffs, getting closer and closer to their destination.

How far away was Eden? Eric wondered. Fifteen miles? Ten? He wasn't sure. His journey to Halawa Bay had been made in stages so that he had no way to judge, and he had long ago lost the map he'd carried. But somehow they had to get there after dark—but not too long after. If they arrived at Eden while it was still light, they would surely be seen. If they had to sail through the rocks and reefs in the darkness, they might never make it. Eric watched Kala, expertly managing the tiller with his good arm, and saw his worried eyes as they studied the course of the little boat. There was a strong, steady breeze and the water seemed calm—almost unnaturally so. It was comforting to know Kala had sailed this coast many times. Better leave it all in his hands.

The sunset was spectacular. Crimson and scarlet, pink and gold drenched the western sky and lingered after the red rim of the sun had disappeared. "Alison would love this sight," Eric mused to himself, missing his twin. "The only good thing about the delay in finding Dad is that at least he won't be reporting me dead! I wonder what Gramps is doing about all this disaster? Is there anything anybody can do?"

The last rays of sunlight silhouetted islands of rock lying just ahead of them. One of them looked like the bow of a black ship.

Then Eric remembered. These were the guardians of the bay that led to Eden.

13 • Return to Eden

In the fading light, Kala guided the catamaran outward to avoid the rocky islands surrounding the mouth of the bay. They had arrived at the cove just at twilight, when they wouldn't be seen from Eden as they sailed toward it in the darkness. The timing seemed perfect. But Kala was scanning the calm water, sniffing the air, his head on one side, as though he smelled and heard something the others couldn't.

Finally he spoke. "Something is wrong, for sure."

"What?" Eric strained to hear what Kala was hearing, but there was only the slosh of their boat through the water, the occasional flap of the sail, and the slapping of the waves against the rocks they passed.

"Not sure. But we not go into bay."

Eric was surprised. "Then how will we get into Eden?"

Kala pointed across the mouth of the inlet.

"We land there. Take trail along shore and up cliff. It take longer, but we got plenty of time."

161

Eric could see where Kala pointed, a patch of white against the dark rocks. It was the Harleys' boat, the *Kamalo*, still lying where it had washed up that day he'd found Eden. It reminded him that he should have phoned the Harleys from the ranch to let them know what was going on, but he hadn't even thought of them till now. Well, he would get the motor of the *Kamalo* fixed and get the boat back to them when this was all over. Maybe Noelani would go with him, and she could meet them. They wouldn't make her feel uncomfortable about her scarred face, he knew that.

A frightened shout from Kala brought him out of his reverie, and he looked up just in time to see the mast of the catamaran dipping suddenly toward the water, and feel the deck rising. With a scraping sound it heaved and tipped, and he found himself in the ocean, struggling in panic as the waves closed over him and he sank.

It happened so quickly that at first he couldn't think, but his reactions were instinctive. He struggled upward, felt a heavy, inert mass curling around him and fought it off, reached the surface finally and took a deep breath, then looked around. One of the log pontoons of the boat floated near him. He caught it, threw his arm over it, and saw, close by, the sail, still attached to the mast, sinking gradually, folds of it flopping in the waves. That must have been what he'd bumped into as he tried to surface. But where were the others?

He shouted into the growing darkness, waited, then shouted again. An answering cry came from Kala, "Over here!"

Eric saw an arm raised over the water, and just a few yards beyond that, the rocky ledge of the shore. He let go the log and swam in that direction.

But he couldn't see Noelani. He was nearing Kala,

who was swimming for the shore, but he could see only one head bobbing through the waves. Where was she? Dismayed, he turned toward the open ocean and shouted for her frantically.

Something firm and moving bumped his back. Startled, he swirled in the water to see Noelani swimming right next to him. She smiled briefly to show she was all right, and together they swam after Kala.

It wasn't a long way, and soon they climbed out on the rocks and lay side by side there, catching their breath.

"What happened?" Eric asked Kala when he could speak again. "What turned the boat over like that?"

"We must have hit a rock. Cut right through boat. Didn't see it."

"Yeah," Eric said. "You weren't watching. You were too busy worrying about whatever you thought was wrong." He was irritated, but he didn't really blame Kala. Still, the Hawaiian had acted strangely out there.

Kala sounded irritated, too.

"You no help. You not watch either."

"Well, now the boat's gone," Eric said. "How do we get back to the ranch? What happens if we have to leave Eden fast?"

"Oh, please don't," Noelani pleaded. "Let's not argue. It wasn't anyone's fault. It was an accident. The only thing is—we've lost the boat it took Kala so long to build, and the cat."

"Don't worry, Kala, I'll help you build another boat," Eric said as he sat up and squinted into the darkness, feeling sick. He'd forgotten about Popoki. He scanned the waves, but it was too dark. He couldn't see a thing out there.

"Did you see where she was when the boat sank?" he asked them. Neither of them had. For a while they sat silently, knowing that she must have drowned.

Eric had a brief thought of swimming back those few yards out to the rock that had capsized them. Maybe she'd been able to hang onto a piece of the splintered wreck. But it was black out there, and he knew his chances of finding her would be slim. He felt terrible. Popoki had been a friend. Without consciously realizing it, he'd become very fond of her. She was independent and affectionate, and she'd never caused a bit of trouble through all their adventures. It seemed so wrong, somehow, that she die this way, just a short distance from safety.

Noelani touched his arm softly.

"Maybe she made it to land, Eric. It wasn't very far—"

"For sure," Kala said without conviction. "That good luck cat. She not dead."

"Maybe you're right," Eric said, and there was silence again.

Kala broke it finally.

"Tide too high. Way too high. That not good. We better go." He got slowly to his feet.

Eric and Noelani got up, too. "Is that what you were so worried about?" Eric asked. "What does it mean?"

"Don't know, but it not good."

Kala began clambering over the rocks, heading for the trail along the cliff, and Eric followed, holding Noelani's hand to help her in the darkness. Kala's obvious fear was catching, making him afraid, too. And who could tell what waited for them in Eden? This trip was going wrong—all wrong. They'd lost their boat, and Popoki, and there was something very strange about the ocean's high tide.

By the time they began their upward climb along the

cliff, the moon appeared, full and bright, casting a silvery glow on their path. They walked without speaking, sometimes stopping to rest briefly because the climb was so steep; always aware that their journey was taking them closer to Eden at every step. Looking at Kala, walking ahead, Eric noticed he'd taken off his sling. He'd probably done that in the water, so he could use both arms to swim to shore. He wondered if Kala believed they'd lost their luck, now that Popoki was gone. He'd always said she was good luck. Oh, how he wished this night was over!

They climbed upward through the rain forest until they came to a place where they could see the ocean again, and the moonlight shining on the shacks of Eden.

Noelani let out a long breath beside him. Kala muttered something that might have been a curse, and they all stood looking at the clearing perhaps a hundred yards away from them.

A fire burned in a circle of stones. Figures passed back and forth around it, and there was the sound of talk and laughter.

"We wait here," Kala whispered. "Got to go through there to get where we go."

"You mean we have to go through Eden to get up to the cliff behind it?"

Eric's skin prickled at the thought.

"For sure. But we not go now. Wait till later."

They sat down on the grass and watched. Eric didn't feel the least bit sleepy. The events of the last hours had left him wide awake.

As the little group at the edge of the rain forest watched the Children of Eden moving around the fire, Kala and Noelani spent the time guessing who they were and pointed them out to each other. "Look, there's

Keala. She's wearing a long muumuu. She must have made a new one.''

"That Lopaka there, he's walking with Malia," Kala observed.

Finally the leaping flames burned down, and one by one the members of the colony disappeared into their shacks for the night, until at last the clearing was empty and silent. Eric judged it must be about midnight, still seven hours to wait for the police to come. He leaned against a tree trunk and closed his eyes, hoping that sleep would come, but his senses were more alert than ever. He moved instantly about an hour later when Kala leaned toward him and said: "We go now."

Walking single file, Kala leading, they moved toward the clearing and stopped at its edge. Kala looked across the glowing fire up toward Pele's house.

"All asleep now," he whispered, "but go fast!"

Then he ran, with Eric and Noelani close behind. Fear gave Eric almost superhuman speed. He knew they would all be killed if someone should see them, but they reached the shelter of the trees on the other side of the clearing without incident.

Eric recognized the trail they had come down the night Kala had rescued him from the shed, and now they went upward, walking quietly. He caught the scent of cooked meat—probably the evening's meal—and once he could smell the odor of the goats that used the path. His neck prickled again as an owl hooted at them, and once a small wild animal scurried across the trail in front of them.

Soon they were behind Pele's house. Kala warned them to be alert here.

Eric held his breath as they passed it.

Did Pele keep her bodyguards, Kimo and Aleka, on

lookout at night? Did she sleep with her windows open? Was she lying in bed listening to them, getting ready to run out and grab them? He let out his breath as they passed beside the shed where he had been held prisoner, and now they were climbing up into the forest again. The danger was past.

Now Noelani took the lead. She walked confidently, as though she knew the way perfectly, and for a while they followed her until they emerged into an open meadow.

Moonlight outlined the cliffs that made a semicircle around it. Eric heard the splash of a waterfall not far away, and smelled the rain-washed foliage of the gentle slope. He was tired enough to sleep now, he knew, so he was glad when Noelani said, "This is it," and sat down on the grass. He seated himself beside her, and Kala followed suit.

"We're safe now," Noelani said. "All we've got to do is wait here."

"Where are the marijuana plants?" Eric tried to see, but couldn't make out much in the distance.

"Over there. And that," Noelani pointed behind them "is the cliff where my parents fell."

Kala, stretched out on the grass, began to breathe regularly.

"Noelani, we should get some sleep now too," Eric said.

"Okay." Her voice sounded weary.

Eric lay back and looked up at the stars that seemed to hang just out of reach above him. It was all right, he thought. They had made it through Eden. The worst was over.

Eric stirred as bright shafts of light glared through his half-opened eyes. His whole body tensed. It was a brilliant, flickering light that nearly blinded him. Someone laughed, and then he felt the pain of something ramming against his back. He sat up.

Pele's face was close to his. She was laughing.

Noelani screamed.

"Get up, *haole*!" Pele screeched.

She kicked her foot against his back.

Kimo and Aleka were there, and they were pulling at Noelani and Kala. Now Pele was telling Eric to stand up. He got quickly to his feet, stumbling a little, backing away from the evil woman who stood before him.

She laughed again. "So you came back to Eden to destroy us, Eric Thorne? You can never destroy Pele!"

Her triumphant smile was ugly, distorted by the light of the torches her two men carried. Eric could see that Kimo held Noelani's neck in the crook of one strong arm, while Aleka had the same grip on Kala.

Pele spoke to all of them. "You should know that Pele sees everything—knows everything. Did you think you could come back to Eden secretly?"

"You're lying," Eric said. "You're just as mortal as the rest of us. You or someone else must have seen us coming up here." His voice shook with fear as he spoke, but he was determined to fight Pele this time—even if he lost.

Her eyes glittered like flames.

"You are foolish, Eric Thorne. You defy powers you know nothing about." She turned to glare at Noelani and Kala, her voice rising with rage. "And you are traitors to your own family. Now tell me, why did you come back here?"

Noelani looked at her with frightened eyes. Kala glowered, but did not speak.

Eric's voice resounded bravely in the silence as he

168

answered for them. "If you know everything, Pele, you should already know why we're here."

"I want you to tell me." The woman nodded to Aleka, who held Kala. "Make him tell," she ordered.

Aleka tightened his grip on Kala's neck and growled, "Answer!"

"Pua'a!" Kala spat the word.

Aleka apparently resented being called names. He brought the torch he held perilously close to Kala's face. "Answer!"

"No," Pele said. "Not yet. I don't want him burned now. If Kala won't tell, Noelani will." She nodded to Kimo. "Make her talk."

Before Kimo could move, Eric jumped at him, chopping at his neck to make him release the girl. Kimo had to let her go. He dropped the torch he was holding with his free hand, and struggled with Eric. It was an uneven fight. Kimo, bigger and heavier than Eric, soon held his neck in a deadly armhold, and his two wrists gripped painfully behind him.

Pele picked up the fallen torch and held it high. With her white hair streaming around her angry face, and her dark piercing eyes, she did look to Eric exactly like the pictures of the volcano goddess he'd seen. A primitive, unreasoning fear grew inside him. He understood now why Kala and Noelani believed her to have powerful *mana*. She was bigger than life, and she was terrifying.

Even her voice was terrifying, rumbling like an earthquake, making him tremble. "I know the reason you are here. It is as I said. You came here to destroy us. But you will be destroyed, instead." She pointed to Noelani with an accusing finger. "You, who bear the mark of the serpent, will die."

The finger swung slowly around to Eric. "And you,

169

haole, are already marked for death—for the *kapu wela.*
You escaped it for a while, but now it will be done.''

She lowered her arm and turned to Kala. ''You
surprise me, Kala. I didn't know you would turn against
us. But now I see that your love for Noelani is very
strong. The serpent has turned your heart against us with
her soft words.''

Noelani, clinging to the trunk of a tree, moaned. It
was a heart-rending sound that stabbed at Eric's heart.

''Noelani is no serpent,'' he shouted at Pele. ''You are
the snake in Eden.''

''So! She wriggled into your heart too?'' Her eyes
widened with fury. *''Kapu wela!''* she screamed. ''You
will all die at dawn in the fire.''

Eric felt Kimo's arm tighten convulsively at his throat.
He squirmed, trying to free himself, but the man who
held him was too strong. It was a moment before Kimo's
grip relaxed enough for Eric to speak.

''If you hurt us,'' he shouted to Pele, ''the police will
know. They're on their way here.''

She whirled to look at him. ''Police?'' Her eyes were
narrowed with suspicion.

''You don't think we'd be stupid enough to come here
alone, do you? They'll be here any minute now, and
they'll be looking for us.''

''You're lying!''

''Wait and see.''

For a moment she stood in silence, staring at him.

Then Kala spoke. ''Eric tell truth. Police come here to
get you.''

Kimo's grip tightened again at Eric's neck and his
voice was furious. ''Let's kill them now, Pele. We kill
them, throw them in fire pit now.''

''No.'' Pele shook her head. ''Wait. If the police come

here and find out—that will be the end. Of everything."
She gave Kimo a meaningful glance. "Everything. You
understand?"

"But gods say they die—" Kimo was trembling,
whether from anger or fear, Eric couldn't tell.

Pele nodded slowly. "Yes. They must die. But the
police must not find them, alive or dead. Even if they're
lying, even if the police aren't coming here, these three
must disappear so nobody will ever know they were
here."

She glanced up at the sky, as though searching there
for some sign, and in spite of himself, Eric looked up
too. Only a canopy of stars, only a misty moon and the
dark cliff. What had he expected? He heard the mocking
hoot of an owl somewhere close, and the distant splash
of water on rocks.

But Pele seemed suddenly satisfied.

"We will take them to the ocean and drown them,"
she announced triumphantly. "Their bodies will be lost
at sea. Nobody will ever know if they were here or not.
And if the police come, they'll need a search warrant.
Let them try to get into Eden without these three to help
them."

Holding the torch high, she grabbed Noelani's arm
and began pulling her down the slope. "Come on! Let's
get them down to the boat. They will be sacrificed to
Mano, the shark goddess."

Aleka shoved Kala ahead of him, and Kimo, still
holding Eric's arms tightly, pushed him along after
them. Eric went reluctantly, knowing there was no
chance to escape now, feeling sorry that he'd tried the
ruse about the police being here soon. He should have
kept his mouth shut. If Pele had tried to throw them into
the fire pit at dawn, the police might have been able to

stop her. He'd made matters worse instead of better.

Pele was taking the path that led around Eden, the same path they'd used coming up here. Apparently, she didn't want the Children of Eden to witness the slaughter. But Eric knew that even if they found out, they wouldn't try to change her mind. The colonists of Eden did whatever Pele told them to do. They were like mindless robots, and she had them in her power.

His thoughts raced, exploring every possibility of escape, but there seemed to be nothing he could do. Even if he could break away from Kimo, his two friends would still be captives. Kala could take care of himself, but Noelani might not be able to. He prayed and searched his mind for a way out of this desperate situation. By the time they'd reached the bottom of the slope and were heading for the water's edge, he still had no plan for escape.

Kimo pushed him over the rocky ground. Pele was still towing Noelani, a few feet ahead of him, and Aleka had Kala by the wrist, forcing him onward, using only one strong hand as he held his torch with the other. In another minute they would be in the motorboat that would take them out on the ocean to their death.

Kimo stopped suddenly. "Look!" he said, surprised. "Look at water!"

Eric seized his chance. Kimo's grip had relaxed slightly, and Eric jerked his arms with a swift judo movement, freeing them from Kimo's grasp. Then he turned and brought his knee up, slamming it into Kimo's groin. The man howled and doubled over with pain, and Eric clasped his hands together and brought them down with all his strength on the exposed back of Kimo's neck, sending him to the ground.

Now he whirled around to see the others. Kala was

struggling with Aleka, and Pele, still holding Noelani, was standing near, looking startled. Taking advantage of her surprise, Eric raced toward her. As she stepped back to get away from him, he put out both hands and shoved her. Then, as Pele staggered off balance, he reached for Noelani's arm to pull her free of the woman's grasp. But Noelani had already sized up the situation. She struggled, elbows and knees lashing out at the woman who still tried to hold her, and freed herself with a triumphant cry. Eric caught her hand, and together they raced across the rocks, hardly feeling the pain of their bruised feet, in their attempt to escape their captors.

There was only one way of escape, that was back up the slope they had come down. Hand in hand, they reached the path and sped upward, panting. Eric heard shouts behind them, but he didn't dare stop and see what was going on. His heart was thumping now, and his breath coming in gasps, but still he pulled Noelani's hand and raced on until he could finally go no farther.

The shore below them was illuminated by moonlight, the three people there sharply defined in light and shadow. Kala was not one of them. But Pele and her two men stood facing the ocean, not moving, making no sound at all. Why weren't they coming up here after them? What was the matter with them?

Then he saw it. Far out in the bay, what looked like a solid wall of water, as high as a tall building, was moving toward the shore. He had never seen anything like it. Too short of breath to speak, he caught Noelani's arm and pointed, so that she could see it, too.

She looked, and her arm under his hand went stiff. When he glanced at her, he saw terror on her face. And through her heavy breathing he caught the syllables of one word she whispered as though it were a death sentence.

"Tsunami!"

14 • Tsunami

Noelani's face turned white under the scar that branded it. She and Eric stood on the slope, frozen by fear, watching Kimo, Aleka, and Pele on the moonlit shore, and the huge wall of water that rolled across the bay toward them.

Suddenly Pele moved with amazing speed. She leaped to the top of a high rock and stood there, facing the ocean, her long dress blowing in the wind, her hair flowing out behind her like a white cloud, and she lifted her arms as though to hold back the sea. Now her voice rose. She seemed to be chanting, crying out a frenzied litany.

He couldn't believe what he saw.

"Is she trying to stop that wave? She's crazy!"

Noelani's voice was hushed. "Maybe she will stop it. She's telling the gods to hold it back."

"She doesn't think—" Eric began, but now he knew that Pele really did believe in her own powers. The woman was some kind of fanatic. "But she can't!" He

176

was dumbfounded. "Her gods are only make-believe. She can't control the ocean!"

The girl looked at him with an odd expression. "If she can't, Eric, that tsunami will kill us all."

Now, for the first time, Eric realized that the gigantic wave, which must be a hundred feet high, was rolling in with such force and speed it would sweep up the slope to where they stood and drag them into the sea. *Tsunami!* Of course! Now he knew he'd heard that word before—heard about the heaving mountains of water, churned up by earthquakes, that had struck the Hawaiian Islands before, nearly destroying whole cities along the coast.

He knew that they should run for their lives, try to get higher up the slope, race all the way to the highest point they could reach to get away from that wave, but he seemed pinned to the spot by the fearsome, fascinating sight. So he stared at the woman standing alone on her pinnacle of rock, arms outflung, trying to hold back the sea.

He heard someone calling him. The sound was urgent, jarring him back to his senses. He looked around and saw Kala's moving figure on the side of the cliff above them, beckoning. "Get over here! Hurry!"

Eric grabbed Noelani's arm and tried to pull her away. With an impatient cry she jerked out of his grasp.

"No!"

"We've got to save ourselves!" He reached for her again.

"Pele! She can save us! She's got to." Noelani squirmed away from him. "They're all asleep, Eric. All the Children of Eden. They'll all die unless Pele holds back that wave."

There was no time to argue with her. Eric took her wrist firmly and pulled her with him through the trees, while Kala urged them to hurry. At first she hung back, but when Eric refused to let her go she finally ran with him on the upward-slanting course toward the cliff. Eric didn't know how they could get up to where Kala was. He only knew they had to reach higher ground somehow.

They were at the bottom of the cliff now, and he saw Kala in the moonlight, pointing down. What was he showing them? Eric searched frantically until he saw a series of narrow rocky ledges, barely visible, that they could climb. He pushed Noelani toward the first one.

"Climb!" he yelled. "Climb up there."

She looked at him for a moment, then nodded silently and let him help support her as she got her foot on the ledge and found the next higher one to climb on. He barely gave her time to get there before he was behind her. In a few moments Kala's hands were reaching down to help her up, and Eric wasted no time clambering after her.

Kala was standing in a shallow niche on the cliff wall, where shoulder-high rocks formed a U-shaped barrier around two sides of the ledge. Eric and Noelani pressed in beside him, and looked over the rocks to the beach below them.

The towering wave had nearly reached the shore. Two figures that must be Kimo and Aleka crouched in positions of terror, looking up at it. Pele, outlined by moonlight, stood on her rocky perch, head flung back, arms raised, crying defiance. The wall of water loomed above her and poised there, while Kimo and Aleka ran across the beach, shrieking, and for a moment time seemed to freeze. Eric saw the foaming dark mass of the wave with frightening clarity, and the sparkle of the rings on Pele's hands raised toward the doom that approached her. He heard her voice screaming a last angry command as the wave engulfed her, swallowed her whole, and rolled on in the sudden silence.

It was coming straight toward them! Eric shouted a terrified warning to the others as he stepped in front of Noelani in a vain attempt to shield her. She screamed in panic and clasped both her arms around his waist. The mountainous wave came swiftly and they saw it curl along the edge of the cliff as it approached. Now it was above them, hovering there for an instant before it fell on them.

Engulfed in a torrent, Eric clung to the rock. In a moment his feet were swept off the ground and his face and chest scraped against the rough stone surface. He held his breath and fought to keep his grasp on the only solid thing he could feel, but his fingers were torn from the rock and he was buffeted against it with such force that it knocked the breath out of his lungs. Now his body tumbled and turned like a piece of seaweed, helpless in the churning wave. Salt water filled his mouth and nostrils. He had to have air! He struggled to push himself upward, to find the surface of the water where there would be air to breathe, but which way was up? He met obstacles everywhere as he bumped back and forth, enclosed in a watery coffin. Once he felt arms and legs entwine with his own, and as he opened his eyes he saw a face like a mask of death, unrecognizable.

He screamed soundlessly and knew no more.

Someone was crying. The sound beat against his ears. Red waves of pain went through him and made patterns in his head. At first he couldn't feel anything else, but gradually he realized his body was lying on something solid, that it felt raw and sore, that his eyes ached and his jaws hurt. He could taste saltwater in his mouth and throat. All life and energy were drained out of him. He could only lie still and feel the pain.

There were soft, sad voices beside him. He knew he should move, open his eyes, and find out who was there, but he wasn't sure where he was or why he couldn't remember anything, so he lay still, breathing heavily.

Someone touched him and called to him in a voice choked with tears. With an effort, he lifted his head.

Darkness was all around, but a faint ray of moonlight shone on the girl who knelt beside him. He remembered her suddenly.

"Eric! You're alive!"

He tried to say something, but a fit of coughing wracked him so that he couldn't speak.

Noelani stared at him, her eyes glowing.

"You're all right!" The words were like a prayer of thanks, and for a moment she smiled. Then her voice grew sad again. "They're all gone, Eric. The wave washed them all away. There's nothing—no one—left."

Eric wasn't sure who she was talking about, but he looked where she pointed and saw a barren strip of ground.

"We thought you were dead," Noelani told him.

He tried to sit up, but fell back weakly.

"Where's Kala?" he managed to ask.

"Here. I'm okay too." Now Eric could see him hunched against the cliff wall in the shadows. "We all about drown."

"We must have caught the very end of the wave," Noelani said. "These rocks kept us from being washed off the cliff."

Now Eric remembered that, too—the terrifying wave that had covered them, and how he had taken saltwater into his mouth and lungs. Why hadn't he drowned?

180

Probably because the wave had washed up over him and then pulled back again, so that he could breathe once more. Unless—

With an effort he managed to get himself into a sitting position against the rock wall.

"Did you give me artificial respiration?" he asked them.

They both looked blank, not seeming to understand. Maybe here in Eden they knew nothing about it.

"We were all unconscious," Noelani told him. "I don't know how long, but Kala and I came around before you did. We're banged and bruised, but I think you got the worst of it. You were right next to the rocks, and Kala and I were behind you. How do you feel?"

"Sore all over." Eric flexed his arms and legs. "I guess nothing's broken, though." He put his fingers up to his face and felt the rough, scraped skin, and the sharp pain in his nose when he touched it. "I'm glad you knew enough to get us up here," he said to Kala.

"Sure. I live here long enough." Kala shook his head somberly. "But Eden all gone. All the Children gone."

Now Eric realized what that barren strip of ground meant. Painfully, pulling himself up by holding onto the rocks, he peered over them. The rain forest—the shacks of Eden—they had all disappeared. There was only the bare slope down to the ocean, where debris littered the shore. And an image came back to him, of Pele standing on a rock, fighting the elements. Now she was gone, and her new Eden was gone too—all taken by the forces she thought she ruled. How tragic it seemed that so many innocent people had died. He surveyed the ruin silently.

"There be more waves come tonight," Kala said behind him. "Water way low now. High waves come again."

"More waves? Are you sure?"

"Right," Kala said. "More waves. Maybe not so big."

"When will they come?"

"Don't know." Kala got to his feet slowly, and Eric noticed that he, too, must be feeling aches and pains, judging by the way he moved. "We go up to high ground now."

"Let's go." Eric felt panic. He had no desire to go through another experience with a tsunami wave. Not ever again. In spite of his sore limbs, he followed Kala, who was climbing down the rocks. Noelani came after them.

They went over the ground licked bare by the tsunami, where only a few large trees remained. Puddles of sea water gleamed in the moonlight. Everything seemed to have been sucked out by the giant wave as it washed back over the devastated land. As they walked, they kept looking back to make sure another wall of water wasn't chasing them, but all Eric could see was a mass of flotsam on the low tide and something that looked like a white boat bobbing in the distance.

On higher ground the going was easier. They passed Pele's house, parts of it still standing like a ghostly reminder of what had been. Kala and Noelani walked past it without saying a word.

Eric was exhausted, his aching body protesting every step of the way, but they had to go on. He knew that. What if an even bigger wave hit them? He wondered what time it was. How many hours would they have to wait for the police? That was their only link with civilization now, and their only way to get away from here. It was still dark, and he had no idea how long he had lain in that niche on the cliff. It might be two o'clock now, or four. What time did the sun rise? Five? Six?

Finally they reached the same open meadow where Pele had found them earlier, and they all collapsed on the ground to rest. Eric stared at the stars with sleepless eyes. It felt good, lying here on the soft grass, but he was wide awake, so he watched the sky and wished for morning.

He heard the next wave as it hit the shore. It sounded, at first, like a soft roll of thunder, becoming the unmistakable noise of lapping, sloshing water that lasted a long time. At least there were no more people who would be destroyed down there. Now they were on high ground where the tsunami couldn't reach them.

Kala and Noelani heard it too.

"Not such big one." Kala seemed positive.

"Maybe the tsunami's just about over now." Noelani's voice was small and wistful.

Eric hoped so, too. This night seemed a hundred years long. Surely it would end soon.

"Listen! Do you hear it?" Noelani asked in the darkness.

Eric held his breath. It was the sound of a motor, coming their way. And there was a beam of light shining in the sky over the land below them.

"The police!" he shouted.

The helicopter was shining a searchlight, looking for them. All three of them jumped up and waved until the beam caught them and the aircraft set down in the meadow close to them. They ran toward it as two uniformed men got out. By the bright lights of the helicopter, Eric saw that one was pleasant-faced and heavily built, the other thinner, with sharp features.

"Which one of you is Eric Thorne?" the heavier man asked them.

Eric went forward. "That's me. And you're Sergeant Lee?"

"I'm Captain Kona. This is Sergeant Lee."

Eric shook hands happily with both of them and introduced Noelani and Kala.

Captain Kona seemed brusque and worried. "Did anyone else escape the tsunami?"

"No," Eric said. "All of Eden was destroyed."

The captain looked astonished. "You were lucky! Stayed right here on high ground, did you?"

Sergeant Lee spoke. "We got news of the seismic waves heading this way and figured we'd better get right over here. We knew you'd be waiting and we hoped you'd be safe. We've got more copters out there, searching." He indicated the ocean with a nod of his head. "Maybe they'll find more survivors."

Eric wanted to tell the whole story but he felt too exhausted. Relief at seeing the police helicopter, at realizing they were safe now, had left him drained. He could only nod silently.

"Well, get into the helicopter," Captain Kona urged them. "We got hold of one big enough for all of us. Let's get you away from here."

Eric felt his spirits reviving as they climbed into the aircraft. Noelani, too, seemed happier, sitting between him and Kala. "I've never been in an airplane before," she said.

Kala grinned, "Me either."

But as they flew down the slope, over the barren place that had once been Eden, they grew sad and silent again. Eric knew how they must feel. Eden had been their home, and the Children of Eden their friends. They had even loved and trusted Pele for a long time. Now everything had been taken away from them.

Captain Kona broke into his thoughts, speaking to Eric over his shoulder. "In all this excitement, I almost forgot. I've got good news for you, Eric. Dr. Thorne has been found."

Eric's heart leaped. "Is he all right?"

"Well—he's alive. He and the pilot of the IAF helicopter were found on Oahu, in a remote corner of the island. They're both injured, but not critically. I believe your father has a broken leg and some cracked ribs. Both he and the pilot are in the hospital here, at Kaunakakai."

Eric felt relief and worry and astonishment, all at once. "How did they get back on Oahu? The volcano and everything?"

"According to what we got out of those two hijackers, they dumped them there, figuring we'd be looking everywhere else for them. Oahu is pretty much of a disaster area right now, you know."

"The hijackers? You caught them?"

"Caught them red-handed. That's how we found out where to look for your dad and the pilot. We spotted the IAF helicopter and brought it down. They were flying it to the Big Island."

Eric still didn't fully understand. "You mean the hijackers took them back to Oahu and left them there, then flew away in the copter?"

"That's right. They apparently pushed them out of the copter. They both might have been killed, but the area had trees that broke their fall."

Eric clenched his fists as anger surged through him.

Noelani laid a hand on his arm and spoke gently in his ear. "It's all right, Eric. Your dad's safe, at least. The police will take care of the hijackers."

Captain Kona must have heard her, for he laughed.

"They're both in for a nice long jail sentence. Hijacking, attempted murder, and illegal drugs."

"Drug charges?" Eric asked, surprised.

"Yes." It was Sergeant Lee who spoke now. "You told us about those orchid leis from Eden, remember? One of the hijackers was wearing an orchid lei when we caught them. We had it analyzed. Found out the rope it was strung on had marijuana in it, all right. You made a good guess."

Eric stared out through the helicopter window, where the dawn was breaking over the ocean. His thoughts raced. The red-haired hijacker had taken that lei from him in the IAF copter that day. Maybe his hunch about him had been right, too. Maybe those two guys were mixed up in the same business as Pele. "Where are we going now?" he asked the captain.

"Back to Kaunakakai. We'll take you to your father in the hospital, and then we need you to identify the two hijackers."

Eric looked at Noelani. "Will you come with me? I think those men might be people you'll recognize. I think those hijackers were two of the men who watched you girls while you were selling the leis. When they saw us talking in the marketplace, and when they saw you give me the orchid lei, they got suspicious and radioed to Pele. That's how she knew about it. Anyway, if they did, then they might have followed Dad and me to the airport that day to keep us from taking that orchid lei to the police."

"Yes," she said thoughtfully. "I think you might be right."

"And if that's the case," Eric went on, thinking fast, "then they'd think we knew all about the marijuana. No wonder they tried to kill me, and Dad and the pilot,

186

too."

Kala was watching the ocean below them. "More waves," he said now, "but not so big."

"How long will this tsunami last?" Eric asked.

Captain Kona answered. "Most of them last two or three hours. The waves build up to a huge height, then they subside. I think this one's about over."

The copter had reached the mouth of the cove, and Eric saw something below him that made him look twice. It was a boat that looked very much like the *Kamalo,* riding the water upright, tossing in the swell. "Could you go lower?" he asked Sergeant Lee, who was piloting the craft. "I think that's my boat down there."

"All right." The copter descended, and by the first rays of the rising sun, Eric could read the name "Kamalo" painted on the side of the boat. It had survived the tsunami even though it had been torn from its anchor, and it looked sound and seaworthy.

Eric felt torn. He wanted to see his dad, but he didn't want to leave the boat like this, tossing among the rocky islands at the mouth of the bay. He should get the *Kamalo* back to the Harleys. It was bad enough that he'd lost Popoki, without losing their boat, too. "I've got to get on her before she's washed out into the open ocean, or smashed on those rocks," he told them, and then he explained about the Harleys and how he'd borrowed the cabin cruiser from them.

Captain Kona objected. "We need you in Kaunakakai. Both you and the young lady, here, will have to identify those men we're holding."

"I'll be there. As soon as I get the engine going again, I'll take the boat to Kaunakakai first and take care of everything there. Then I'll get it back to the Harleys. They're not far from Kaunakakai anyway."

187

"Where are they?" Captain Kona still sounded reluctant.

"At a hotel on the west end of the island. The Sheraton."

"That's not too far away." The captain scratched his nose thoughtfully. "But what about those waves? They don't worry you?"

"No," Eric said. "I've handled a boat before on a stormy sea. I think I could do it all right now, if I can get that motor going again."

"It's probably had time to dry out by now," Sergeant Lee said, "if it was only water in the engine. That is, if the tsunami didn't foul it all up again. But the boat must have stayed on top of the waves, so she'd keep dry enough. That's happened before in tsunamis. Boats can ride the waves. It's the land that is destroyed."

Unexpectedly, Kala spoke eagerly, "Let's go. We get her started."

Captain Kona raised his eyebrows. "You know anything about engines?"

"For sure. I work on boats at Eden. Eric and me, we get *Kamalo* going."

"We-l-l-l—all right. I guess you can't just leave her drifting around out here." The captain glanced down at the boat, frowning. "But you've got to promise to be in Kaunakakai without fail." He turned to the sergeant. "We brought that rope ladder for rescue, didn't we?"

"It's in the back."

Eric looked at Noelani. "Want to come with us?"

She nodded, smiling. "Of course."

The sergeant brought the helicopter down and hovered over the *Kamalo,* and Eric, Noelani, and Kala went down the rope ladder to the deck. They waved to the two policemen as the copter whirled away, then looked happily at each other. It was good, Eric thought, that the three of them were alone together again. They'd been through so much it seemed natural, now.

"Come on," he said, "let's take a look at the engine."

Kala was already peering at the engine, and in a moment he reached in and pulled out a thick clump of seaweed, disentangling it from the rotors. "Here. This your trouble," he said triumphantly.

And at that moment, as he was examining the clump of seaweed, feeling embarrassed that he hadn't found it himself, Eric heard a sound behind him. Was he hearing things? Before he could turn, something soft rubbed against his back, and the sound came again—a joyful sound that was half-purr and half-meow.

"*Popoki*?" He looked around.

Eyes closed, tail up, the cat pushed against him.

"How did *you* get here?" Eric almost lost his balance.

With a cry of joy, Noelani picked her up and hugged her, while Kala stood shaking his head in disbelief.

For a moment they could only babble in surprise and pleasure while Popoki purred in response.

"Maybe she really can swim," Eric suggested.

"Or maybe she climbed onto a piece of the wrecked boat," Noelani said. "Then she would have been pushed to shore by the waves."

"Like I said," Kala grinned, "she good luck cat."

Eric laughed. "Yeah, she's lucky for herself as well as us—lucky that the *Kamalo* was right there. She must have found it and hidden in the cabin during that tsunami."

Noelani nodded. "That's the only way she could have survived it. But I guess we'll never know for sure just how she made it." She set Popoki down on the deck.

"She seems to be okay, but I'll bet she's hungry. Is there any food for her?"

"Nope," Eric said. "She's going to have to wait for her breakfast till we get to Kaunakakai, just like the rest of us."

After a couple of tries, Eric got the engine started and soon he was steering the *Kamalo* around the rocks at the mouth of the cove. Noelani stood near him, watching the pink and gold sunrise, and Kala sat on the deck beside them, with Popoki at his feet. Eric felt happier than he'd been for days. Everything seemed perfect. Even his cuts and bruises weren't bothering him much. But in a couple of hours they'd be docking at Kaunakakai. Then what? He'd have to stay with Dad, at least until he was able to get around by himself.

He looked at Noelani—at her lovely dark eyes, and her flowing black hair and the ugly scar on her cheek—the terrible memento of her days in Eden. What would happen to her now?

She caught his glance and reddened slightly, putting her hand up quickly to cover the scar. "I forget about it sometimes now. Does it look very bad?"

"*You* look beautiful," he said truthfully. "You'll see a plastic surgeon, won't you?"

She nodded. "I've been thinking about—about what I'll do now. I think I'll go back home for a little while."

"Home?" At first Eric thought she meant Eden.

"To my aunts and uncles. They wanted to send me to school a long time ago—before I went to Eden. I think now I'll go. I'd like to go back to school. And there's so much of the world I want to know about—so many things to see and do."

Kala looked up at her. "I go too, Noelani. Lots of things I want to learn."

190

She smiled at him. "Okay. Maybe we can go to the same school, Kala." She turned the smile to Eric. "Now that I know Pele was wrong, that Hawaii isn't going to be destroyed, it seems as though everything's new and beautiful. I don't know how I could have believed her for so long."

She looked happy and radiant, and Eric longed to tell her how much he loved her, but there was Kala, sitting right there watching him. And Kala loved her too. The situation was just the same with the three of them. He still couldn't tell which of them Noelani liked best.

Then he had an idea. He could get Noelani alone, without having Kala around. "I'm going to be here the rest of the summer," he told her, "and I haven't seen much of Hawaii yet. How about showing me around the islands?"

"I'd like that," she said. "I can show you some great places."

Kala looked at both of them and grinned. "For sure. We all spend summer together."

The *Thorne Twins* Adventure Books
by Dayle Courtney

#1—*Flight to Terror*
Eric and Alison's airliner is shot down by terrorists over the African desert (*2713*).

#2—*Escape From Eden*
Shipwrecked on the island of Molokai in Hawaii, Eric must escape from the Children of Eden, a colony formed by a religious cult (*2712*).

#3—*The Knife With Eyes*
Alison searches for a priceless lost art form on the Isle of Skye in Scotland (*2716*).

#4—*The Ivy Plot*
Eric and Alison infiltrate a Nazi organization in their hometown of Ivy, Illinois (*2714*).

#5—*Operation Doomsday*
Lost while skiing in the Colorado Rockies, the twins uncover a plot against the U.S. nuclear defense system (*2711*).

#6—*Omen of the Flying Light*
Staying at a ghost town in New Mexico, Eric and Alison discover a UFO and the forces that operate it (*2715*).

Available at your Christian bookstore or from Standard Publishing.